Francis B Nyamnjoh
Stories from Abakwa
Mind Searching
The Disillusioned African
The Convert
Souls Forgotten

Dibussi Tande
No Turning Back. Poems of Freedom 1990-1993

Kangsen Feka Wakai
Fragmented Melodies

Ntemfac Ofege
Namondo. Child of the Water Spirit

Emmanuel Fru Doh
Not Yet Damascus
The Fire Within

Thomas Jing
Tale of an African Woman

Peter Wuteh Vakunta
Grassfields Stories from Cameroon

Ba'bila Mutia
Coils of Mortal Flesh

Kehbuma Langmia
Titabet and The Takumbeng

Ngessimo Mathe Mutaka
Building Capacity: Using TEFL and African languages as development-oriented literacy tools

Milton Krieger
Cameroon's Social Democratic Front: Its History and Prospects as an Opposition Political party, 1990-2011

Sammy Oke Akombi
The Raped Amulet
The Woman Who Ate Python & Other Stories

Francis B Nyamnjoh & Richard Fonteh Akum
The GCE Crisis: A Test of Anglophone Solidarity

PRECIPICE

Susan Nkwentie Nde

Langaa Research & Publishing CIG
Mankon, Bamenda

Publisher:
Langaa RPCIG
(*Langaa* Research & Publishing Common Initiative Group)
P.O. Box 902 Mankon
Bamenda
North West Province
Cameroon
Langaagrp@gmail.com
www.langaapublisher.com

ISBN: 9956-558-17-6

DISCLAIMER
All views expressed in this publication are those of the author and do not necessarily reflect the views of Langaa RPCIG.

Content

1

The crowd outside the casualty department grew larger as news went round town that a bus had fallen down the station hill in Bamenda town. Some people were wondering whether to go to the scene of the accident or to go to the hospital. At the scene of the accident, a crowd was still gazing with unbelieving eyes at the wreckage. The bus was bashed on all sides and splinters of glass were scattered on the hillside. The onlookers wondered how anybody could have come out of it alive.

At the hospital, the fourteen passengers who had been on board were in various stages of shock. The reception was full with casualties. In the inner room, two of the very bad cases were lying on the two available beds. The rest were on the floor while some sat on the benches outside. Those who were conscious enough to speak recounted the incident. The narration was interrupted often with groans of pain. The nurses discouraged the casualties from speaking too much but the excitement and the shock of the incident was too much for them to keep quiet. There were exclamations and sighs from the audience.

From the versions that passed from lip to lip, it was finally established that while the bus was being loaded at the Nkwen bus stop, the driver was busy drinking in a nearby bar. It was even said that at one point when he was called to settle a problem concerning a passenger who had refused to pay an additional sum of five hundred francs for his luggage, he had rushed out in anger and, without asking what the man wanted to give, had asked him to pay or get out of his bus. He had come along with his unfinished bottle of Export beer from which he sipped as he spoke. When the passengers complained about his drinking and driving, he asked them to get down if they were afraid of dying.

When the bus was full, he took off with such speed that the passengers looked at each other. At the outlet of the bus stop, a woman asked the driver to stop so that she could buy a bottle of Supermont for her baby. In response to her request, she got a barrage of recriminations from her fellow passengers and particularly from the driver. They asked why she had not bought it when they were still at the bus stop and the bus had not yet taken off. Women were such nuisance, some of the passengers complained. The passengers were divided into two camps with the majority taking sides with the woman for they were disgusted with the uncompromising attitude of the driver. Fortunately the bus was by the Total Petrol Station so the mineral water could be bought without anybody getting out of the bus. One of the workers at the petrol station was kind enough to bring the bottle of water to the bus and collected the money. When this was done the driver sped up the incline towards the Finance Roundabout seemingly delighted at the discomfiture that reigned among the passengers. He aggravated the situation by making annoying remarks.

The Bamenda Station Hill is a test of the ability of drivers and many a learner driver has failed the driving test on this hill not from lack of skill but from fright. From the hill, the town is seen lying in a valley. It is beautiful scenery with rolling hills in the background. But from the road winding down the hill it looks like an abyss. Many drivers coming to Bamenda for the first time especially in the night have been forced to leave their vehicles up the hill and take a taxi down to town.

The driver, excited by the state of tension among the passengers because of the argument, wanted to frighten them further to keep them quiet. So he sped up the hill, his hands firmly gripping the steering wheel. He focused his gaze on the road. As he negotiated the second bend, he was right in the middle of the road. An oncoming vehicle flashed its lights for him to keep to his own side of the road. He swerved the bus, miscalculated the width of the road and sent the bus rolling down the hill. No passenger came out as the bus somersaulted and was battered on all sides.

As taxis deposited the victims at the hospital, nurses came with stretchers and wheel chairs to evacuate them. The trauma was of various degrees. There were fractured legs and arms, lacerated stomachs and backs, swollen heads and faces, abrasions and multiple injuries. It was a ghastly sight. Blood had thickened into dark smearing on some bodies and some were still bleeding. There was a young man who lay so still that to the layman's eyes, the doctor was coming in his case just to write the cause of death and the other jargon that goes with their profession. He was in a coma and was taken to the reanimation ward. In his condition nothing could be done except the assessment of his visible injuries. In the theatre, the doctors were busy cleaning and stitching wounds.

In the reanimation ward, the nurses were busy too. Since the patient was in no condition to give any information on how he felt, the necessary medical precautions had to be taken. His eyelids were opened and his pupils examined. His fingertips and the soles of his feet were pricked to assess the level of comatose. His case was considered semi-comatose because he responded weakly to the applied pain. A nurse was stationed near him to take note of any changes. His temperature and pressure were taken at intervals.

The radio station had broadcasted the names of the passengers who were in the bus. Now the hospital was full with relatives, sympathizers and those who were just inquisitive. Nobody enquired about the young man who lay in the reanimation ward. A patient in the reanimation ward is a cause for concern but the onlookers at the windows were just inquisitive to know who he was. News was already going round that there was an unknown young handsome man lying in the ward. He was still in his clothes and lying on his back. He was very fair in complexion with high cheekbones. His nose was aquiline. The thin line of moustache on his upper lip gave the impression that he was a teenager just entering into manhood. He had a head of hair and the thin strip that descended on both sides of his face gave it a striking appearance. It was such an arresting face that even in repose, it commanded a second look. The mouth in mobility was sensuous but was now held firmly in place, maybe from pain or the will to live. His shirt was open at the chest and revealed a very fair and unblemished skin, with a thin layer of hair evenly spread on it. He was lying there,

3

oblivious of everything going on around him. Every plan of his was at a standstill waiting for providence to give him the strength to continue.

Ralph Essin had arrived Cameroon two weeks ago from France. Though his only parent, his mother, was living in Yaounde, he had decided to come to Bamenda first to see his best friend with whom he had attended the University of Yaounde. Having been out of the country for five years, he thought it was best for him to make contact with somebody who understood him and would guide him through the transitory period of readjustment before he got caught up in the arms of his mother and the extended family. He had spent a wonderful week in Bamenda and was on his way to Yaounde when tragedy struck.

His friend Russell, with whom he had spent the week, had left the previous day for Yaounde to do some work for his boss and also to see how far his documents had gone in the Ministry of Finance. He had been working for five years and had not yet been integrated into the civil service. He could not wait to travel with his friend because he was travelling with other colleagues in a service vehicle. Their plan was to meet in Yaounde so that Russell could be introduced to Ralph's mother, so that whenever Ralph wanted to come to Bamenda, his mother would not wonder with whom he was going to stay. Ralph wanted his re-entry into the Cameroonian society to be smooth. Though his mother had done everything to secure him a job in Yaounde, he did not want to be tied to her apron strings. He did not want to stay with her for fear she would fuss over him as if he was still mama's boy. While in France, his mother had always written to him about getting married and having children. Being an only child the mother's fears were justifiable. He knew that his mother was going to introduce as many girls as possible to him, – those she thought good enough for him. She might have even chosen one for him already. Ralph was planning to avoid all of these as much as possible. But in this state, whatever the future had for him would wait.

"Good morning, Doctor."

"Good morning, how is the patient?" the doctor asked as he looked at the chart and report in the patient's file.

4

"The patient stirred at about one-thirty a.m. and mumbled some words. Since then he has not stirred again."

"Did he utter any comprehensive words?"

"No Doctor, I could not make sense out of what he was saying."

The doctor scratched the patient's palm and moved it away. With his fingertips, he pulled aside his eyelids. They fluttered and closed again. He started talking to the patient.

"How are you feeling? Do you hear me? Lift up your arm."

He did everything to get the patient to open his eyes. Ralph only moved his head to one side and groaned. The doctor asked the nurses to take his temperature and pressure again. His temperature was rising but his pulse rate remained the same. When the thermometer was withdrawn from his armpit, it showed thirty-nine degrees centigrade. There was something wrong. The nurses became more alert and attentive. In this state it was difficult to get any clue except after another examination. The doctor lifted Ralph's head then he gently placed it on the pillow. He lifted his right hand, then the left. There was no response from the patient. He examined the stomach and tapped it with his fingers. It was not swollen. He moved down to the legs. When he lifted the left leg the patient gave a groan. He let the leg down gently. He lifted it again. The patient stirred, groaned and sighed. On closer examination, there was some discoloration on the left leg along the shine bone. This was a sure sign of a fracture. The leg was immediately put into a splint and tired firmly with a bandage before the patient was taken for x-ray. The film showed a commuted fracture on the femoral shaft. The leg had to be operated upon. Everything was done to bring the patient back to full consciousness. His response to questions was haphazard. This state of amnesia did not last very long however. He opened his eyes soon after and looked around lazily. In a slurred voice, his first coherent utterance was "Where am I?"

"You are in a hospital ward. You are going to be alright," replied the nurse on morning duty.

"What happened? Why am I here?"

5

He tried to get up but could not. The nurse looked at him and felt sad. Ralph reminded her of her son who was studying in Britain and she imagined him in such a situation with nobody to take care of him. She started preparing her patient for the theatre by telling him what was about to be done to him. This psychological preparation is very important as the mental state of a patient affects the healing process. She answered his questions in a manner to put him at ease, and to make him know that he was in good hands and that everything was being done to get him well again. While applying the Sav-On cleansing lotion, she explained in a motherly way that they were just going to take the pain away from the leg. In the theatre, local anaesthesia was applied to the limb and a screen was placed in a position to keep the operating area away from his view. While the operation was going on, the attendant nurses conversed with him and he never knew what was happening to his leg. The doctor made a deft incision. The bone particles were big enough to be easily reset. The use of internal fixation with tiny screws with the help of antibiotics to prevent infection was being tested in the medical field. The doctor drew the attention of his attendants when he was putting the particles of bone in place. Thereafter, a complete immobilization of the leg was necessary. The application of plaster of Paris did not take long and soon Ralph was being wheeled to the New Private Ward.

It was Ralph's first day in the hospital, the first because the previous day had not existed for him. He began wondering how long he was going to stay in the hospital and what was going to become of him. He lay in a pensive mood with his leg throbbing with pain. He touched it. It was hard. He tried to lift it and discovered that it was heavy and painful. With a sigh of resignation he lay back on the bed. The plate of sandwich and cup of tea, which the hospital kitchen had provided, stood on his bedside cupboard untouched. He was thinking of the forces that must have landed him in this fix. He recalled the events of the previous day. He had been surprised at the behaviour of the driver but had not taken part in the argument in the bus. During the arguments he had no choice but to keep his fingers crossed and pray to get to Yaounde safely. But here he was from no fault of his. He thought of the bus services in Europe and realized that his country still had a long way to go.

What was his mother going to say? He wondered. It was terrible to come all the way from France to be maimed in his own country. He knew his mother was not only going to be angry by this fact but also with the fact that he had not come directly to Yaounde but to a friend whom she did not know.

His next thought was to be transferred to a hospital in Yaounde where he would be near his mother who would take care of him. But his mother did not know what had befallen him. He rang the bedside bell to call the nurse on duty. She came running, thinking there was something wrong.

"How are you feeling, Is the leg paining much?" she asked these questions as she walked into the room. The nurses, most of them young women, were already attracted to him and fussed over him.

"I just wanted to send a message to my mother in Yaounde to inform her about my accident, is there a phone I can use?"

"At the moment, the hospital phone does not go out of town. But you can send a radio message." As they were talking, a policeman walked into the room with a suitcase.

"Are you Mr. Ralph Essin?" he asked.

"Yes, Ralph replied and tried to get up. The sudden change in events in his life had made him forget about material things. He had been more concerned with his life. The sight of the suitcase brought back everything.

"Is this your suitcase?" the man asked.

"Yes," Ralph replied. "How did you get it? Thank you so much. I had forgotten completely about it."

The policeman looked at him with a smile. "Please sign here," he said.

The nurse explained later that he was a police from the department of public security and they took care of situations like the one he was involved in.

"Thank you very much," Ralph repeated as the policeman walked out. This assured him that his country was not as backward as he had thought.

7

"Please open the suitcase and give me my dairy and a pen." She opened the suitcase after struggling with the lock for some time. She took out the dairy and pen, brought round the movable dinning table across the bed and helped him to sit up and write.

"I would be very grateful if you would give this at the Radio house for me. When are the announcements made?" She looked at her watch.

"It is ten minutes to two. I have to end my shift at 2 o'clock. The announcements are made at three thirty. If you hurry, I will be able to give it in and it will be read this afternoon. Let me see if my colleagues have come to take over."

With this, she walked out. Left alone he wrote, calling on his mother to come to his aid. He also informed his friend Russell who had travelled to Yaounde the previous day about his predicament. When the nurse returned, she was with two other nurses. They were to take over duty from two to 9 pm. The handing over formality was done. His situation was briefly appraised. The nurse explained the treatment that had been given since morning and what was left to be done. The nurse who had come in last stood with her attention more on the patient than on what was being said. She felt something in her rise and fall. The nurse of the morning shift was already used to his disarming smile. Elise found it enchanting. After all the information had been given, the morning nurse asked for the announcement. It was handed over with some money folded in it. When she discovered this she handed it back to him.

"It is all right. I will hand in the announcement. You do not need to worry. I live up station and the radio house is on my way home."

Ralph found it very unusual for services to be rendered without remuneration. Also he was not aware that his physical qualities could make people, especially women, do things for him. In spite of all his persuasions she refused the money. Before leaving she said, "I am leaving you in very good hands. Sister Pamela and Elise will take good care of you. Stay well." She smiled at him and walked out. He turned to look at the newcomers. The first nurse was in her early thirties and had a tendency to the fat side. The second was younger. The second nurse looked at the patient's file, while the first checked his drugs, tucked him in and tried to make him comfortable. Elise, the second nurse, realized that she was not showing enough interest in the patient, as she should. She had to act hostess to the welcomed guest. She smiled at him and called him by his first name as she had seen it in his file. She made small conversation to put him at ease and to make him like his environment.

"Ralph how is the leg?" She asked moving nearer to the bed. The voice sounded like music in his ears. When she held his arm for his pulse to be taken, the contact was electric.

"Ralph, Ralph, Ralph," she kept saying to herself. The combination of Rs and Ls produced a pleasant sensation in her mouth and being.

"How are you feeling generally?" she asked as she pressed her fingers on his wrist while looking at her watch. She glanced from it, their eyes met and held. For some seconds, she could not take her eyes away. He seemed hypnotized. A smile gradually broke across his face and hers responded in turn, breaking into a broad smile and revealing a set of white teeth. The contrast was stunning, pure white teeth on a dark face. When she smiled at him his heart missed a beat. What a beautiful woman, he thought, very dark in complexion with ivory white teeth. There was a dimple on her left cheek when she smiled. Her dark colour seemed to glow and the hair on her arms was smooth. She was known in her class as the Ashanti Doll. From her hairline, he knew that she had very good hair, and her nurse's cap looked like a halo on her head. He took in all these attributes while she talked to him. But he was not the type of man to fall for a woman because of her physical appearance.

"Try and sleep much. Sleep is the best healer. You will surely need lots and lots. Let me not disturb you. I will be coming again to check on you." As she turned to go he held her hand.

"Pamela."

"I am Elise," she replied smiling at his error.

"I am sorry I called you a different name. Elise, something tells me you are going to take good care of me."

9

"Of course, that is what I am here for, to take care of patients. I hope that I am going to do my best."

The name Pamela had been called when the other nurse was on her way back from the other room where she had gone to see another patient. On hearing her name she turned and looked at Elise and asked.

"Have you been telling him my name?"

"Why should I tell him your name? He thought my name was Pamela. So I was explaining to him it's not."

How did he get to know the name?"

"Did you not hear Sister Cathy saying that Sister Pamela and Elise would take good care of him? I am sure that is when he got the names but he did not know who was who."

Ralph had watched and listened to the exchange between the two nurses. He admired Elise's composure in answering the questions. Sister Pamela's questions were enough to make Elise lose her temper, but she did not. The situation was even at Sister Pamela's advantage as it helped her avoid the uncomfortable situation of a patient directly asking a nurse's name. On going out Sister Pamela noticed the tea tray on the cupboard.

"What! You have not eaten? The sandwich is still there and the tea too. It is cold and the bread is hard. Is there anybody to bring you food?"

I have nobody. I do not know anybody in Bamenda. My people are in Yaounde. I was not hungry but now I am.

"Can you still eat the sandwich?"

"No I cannot. Can you get me something else to eat?" The nurses looked at each other. Elise was touched by his situation. She was also intrigued by his not having anybody in Bamenda.

"Who were you staying here with? Why is the person not here? They should have heard of your misfortune. Did you not inform them?"

"The person I was staying with has gone to Yaounde. I was on my way to meet him there. I hope he'll hear my announcement."

This was a distraction to the problem at hand and Ralph wanted something to eat.

As if to reemphasize the gravity of the situation, his stomach rumbled.

"I am really hungry."

There is nothing we can do. But I think some fruits will keep you going until we can get some food for you."

"Then I will have to go without food till evening," he complained, the spoilt child in him rearing its ugly head. "Can't you get me something to eat? Having stayed for long without food, I would like something liquid first."

He had not bothered where the food was going to come from. All that mattered was that he wanted food to eat. The nurses were on duty and could not leave the hospital. Back at their station they decided to take a risk. Elise offered to rush to a restaurant outside the hospital and buy some food. But they had no dish to put the food in. Elise had an idea. She went to one of the patients, who had just eaten, and asked if she could use his dish. She took it and washed it at her station. She went out and was back with the food. She begged for a spoon from the same patient and was soon in Ralph's room. He was surprised to see her back with food so quickly. It was pepper soup with some plantains.

"How did you get the food? I hope it is good."

"I cannot bring you food that is not good. I know the woman who has cooked it. She cooks well. We often buy food from her."

"I trust you Elise. How much is the food?"

"Eat before you ask. You may lose your appetite."

She helped to bring the movable table nearer and over the bed. Then she held him to sit up. "Now you can eat. Bon appetit." She made to go out.

"Sister please eat with me."

"I am sorry, I can't. I am on duty and I have to go. Moreover the food is so small. It may not be enough for you now that you are so hungry."

Elise had acted on impulse. She had not asked herself why she was so concerned about this young man. She was not attracted by the fact that he was just from France. Something about the young man had touched her. But her colleague

11

thought differently. "Elise, it seems as if you have fallen for that man."

"Why do you say so? I am just being kind to him. Can't you help somebody who is desperate?" Then she remembered that she had not allowed Ralph to pay for the food. She had bought the food for him and was happy that she had done so but was afraid to tell a lie if her colleague asked. She wanted it to be a secret between Ralph and herself. "I see," Sister Pamela responded. "I was just being inquisitive. You are a good woman."

2

*R*alph's announcement went over the air during the Luncheon Date announcements. Though many people heard it, it passed as news usually does if it does not concern you. Russell almost collapsed when he heard it. He was sitting in a stall where food was sold near the Ministries of National Education and Public Service. The whole morning had been spent moving from one room to another, from one floor to another, depositing the documents he had brought from Bamenda and collecting the ones he had to take back. He had also spent much time with the director working on some of the documents he had brought from Bamenda. After that he had gone immediately to the Ministry of Public Service to see how far his integration documents had gone. He was one of the one thousand five hundred university graduates who had been absorbed into the public service.

Chasing documents was a phenomenon which no civil servant could escape. Some documents were dumped in drawers and declared missing. Sometimes they were deliberately hidden for the owner to grease the elbow before they would reappear. This was Russell's fate. He had sent a friend to check on these documents and he had come back with the information that they could not be found. He knew the room in which he had deposited the documents and the person to whom he had given them. So he was sure that his documents were not missing. Russell had just ten thousand francs with him and this was to take care of his transport fare back to Bamenda.

The lady selling the food was aware of the fact that her clients were civil servants and provided a radio for them to listen to the afternoon announcements, news and appointments on the days that this was done. When Russell heard the announcement Ralph had sent, he abandoned the bottle of beer he was drinking. The stall was so noisy that nobody noticed when he left.

He walked back to the Ministry of Public Service. The doors were not yet opened. He loitered impatiently, a tensed expression on his face. He clasped and unclasped his palms in frustration. He was seething with anger at the manner in which the documents of civil servants were treated in his country. All these inner tribulations were leading him nowhere. He calmed down and waited. He looked round and tried to distract himself from his troubles. What he saw was a picture of human misery. What he heard was not consoling. Aged men who could have been in their villages enjoying their much deserved retirement were sitting on benches with their caps off revealing their domes. He could see tiredness and resignation carved on their faces. The doors began to open and the waiters tramped in. A stream of human bodies was soon moving up and down the stairs of the eight-storey building. They were just moving bodies because their minds were elsewhere. Russell cVictoriad to room 603 where he had left his documents the last time he was in Yaounde. He was told that they had been moved to room 706. He had to climb another flight of stairs. He arrived at the landing panting. Not many people were waiting in the corridors and this made him believe his ordeal was soon going to end. When he got to room 706 the door was still closed. Two other men had got there before him. He joined them to wait. He was too tired for conversation and only grunted a greeting, which was not acknowledged. His stomach grumbled in protest, for his food the whole morning had been a stick of soya and half a bottle of beer. Hunger and fatigue was making him dizzy. He looked for a banister to lean on. This brought him closer to the two men who were also waiting. What they were saying started the butterflies fluttering in Russell's stomach. One was telling the other how he had to give the sum of ten thousand francs for his integration documents to be given to him. This was the final room. But before his documents got to this room he had already spent the sum of twenty thousand francs. Russell listened with bewilderment. He was afraid that he must have been misdirected. Maybe his documents were not yet there because he had not spent that sum of money. He wondered what he was going to do if he would have to give ten thousand francs to be given the documents, signed by the competent authority. He would collect his decision but would have no money to pay his fare back to Bamenda. He planned a strategy.

The door swung open from inside and a woman walked out. Russell did not wait a minute. He did not care about the etiquette of first come. He knocked and without waiting for a reply went in. "Good afternoon sir…" he began. The man sitting in the room rattled off in French. Russell could only pick out a few common words and phrases in such circumstances, like: dossier, pas trouvé, demain.

Russell sat down opposite the man without being invited to do so. He pulled out the ten thousand francs note from his pocket and placed it on the table. He looked at the man then he said, "C'est tout. Mon frere mort Bamenda." With gestures he asked the man to take his share and give his and that he had to get back to Bamenda that evening. While saying this perspiration covered his forehead and his eyes were moist. How could a man be brought to such humiliation through no fault of his? He thought as he watched to see what the man was going to do. The man stared straight at Russell. Russell stared back at him without blinking. It was a battle of wills and Russell won. The man lowered his gaze, tapped his fingers on the table and then he got up. He went over to a drawer, pulled out some papers clipped together and placed them before Russell. He looked at them and nodded his head in agreement. The man signed and wrote something on them. He asked Russell to take them to the secretariat for the official stamp and date. All this time he did not look at the money lying on the table. When Russell had the documents in his hands, he looked at the money and then at the man. The man followed his glance and waved him out. Russell picked up the money and with a polite thank you put the money in his pocket and walked out. In the next room the documents were stamped and dated. As he walked out Russell heaved a sigh of relief. He could not believe his luck though it had cost him some of his pride.

Russell looked at his watch. It was eight pm on the dot. The bus was rumbling over the Sananga Bridge and this woke him. Exhausted from the tension of the day and from hunger, the movement of the bus had lulled him to sleep. The sleep and the plate of rice and stew he had eaten at the bus stop refreshed him a bit. Feeling himself again, his thoughts turned to his friend Ralph. He was anxious to get to Bamenda to see the state in which his friend was. The announcement had been read over the evening news again and this brought all sorts of pictures to his mind. He imagined Ralph with a swollen face with his arm in a sling. The he imagined him with stitches all over his body. Russell was a victim of all the extremes to which our imaginations can take us. This was more depressing as the imagined deformities grew more grotesque.

He turned his thoughts to more pleasant things, particularly the nights he had spent with Ralph in Bamenda. He remembered when they went to the Njang Night Club at the Ayaba Hotel. They had taken along two girls. One was his girlfriend and the other was her friend, just to keep the equation balanced and keep off speculators. Ralph was so effusive in his appreciation of the warmth and camaraderie around him that he let go by patting the girl's buttocks and planting kisses on her jaws and forehead. This had brought hilarious laughter from the girl and a smile from her friend. Russell, knowing his friend, was afraid the girl would take him seriously. The money he spent each of the evenings they went out spotted him out as a been-to. What had really impressed Russell about his friend was the fact that for the one week they spent together his friend had never expressed the desire for intimate female relationship though he openly admired the girls. Maybe it was because of the AIDS scare but Russell was not convinced that was the reason. So he once picked him up on the issue.

"Whoa! Ralph, you are strange."

"What do you mean?"

"You just look at the chicks around and you say nothing."

16

"What do you want me to say? Well if you have a suggestion, make it for I have not seen any that is of my taste yet. What about AIDS? Have you forgotten about it?"

"There are still some clean girls."

How do you know that a girl is clean?

"Well, that is the problem," Russell concluded and allowed the topic to drop. He thanked God that he had not encouraged any girl to get close to his friend. He could have regretted it and this would have created a shadow on their friendship.

Madam Essin was not in Cameroon. She had gone to Cotonou to buy goods for sale. Her son had telephoned that he was coming back home but was not definite about his date of arrival. This was partly because he wanted to avoid the family fuss at the airport with flowers and kisses. These were things he could not stand. Also, there was congestion at the airport for it was summer with many people moving to other countries. Flights to Cameroon were all booked for that week.

Her business was flourishing and she too wanted to take advantage of the reduced transportation fare at the beginning of the summer holiday. She had left Cameroon three days before her son arrived and she was to stay for two weeks to buy and collect all the things she wanted to bring home. Many of her friends had ordered for particular items of clothing and jewellery and she had to wait for them to be delivered. She was a successful woman with a son who was already a man. She considered herself ripe enough to have a daughter-in-law and grandchildren. Her son already had a job waiting for him in the Ministry of Finance. He had been educated in one of the best universities in France as an accountant. She had seen to all these. Her plan for a big welcome party was in place. She just wanted to get home, get in touch with her son, know his date of arrival and set her plans rolling.

Russell arrived in Bamenda at one am. He went straight to the hospital, explained the reason for his late visit to the night watchman and left his identity card. At the nurse's station, he explained who he was and was taken to see Ralph. Ralph was sleeping peacefully under the influence of a sedative. The lights and footsteps did not wake him up. Russell was advised to come in the morning. The sight of his sleeping friend and the knowledge he had gained from the nurses had calmed him down. He went back to his house, kept his bag on one of the chairs, removed his coat and shoes and fell on the bed. It was eight o'clock the next day when he opened his eyes and pulled off the blanket from his body. The rays of the sun were streaming in through the window where the blinds had not been properly closed. He hurriedly took a bath, drank a cup of coffee and rushed to the hospital. He arrived when the doctor was in Ralph's room checking on his operated leg and discussing his situation with the nurses. This was taking some time so Russell decided to stroll around before coming back. When he went back the doctor had gone. He was surprised on entering the room to find a beautiful girl dishing fish pepper soup into a bowl for Ralph. There was a plate of bread and farmer's omelette on the cupboard. There was also an empty teacup. Ralph and this girl were laughing at a joke he had missed. He felt relieved because on his way to the hospital, he had been wondering how his friend was going to be fed. The bachelor food he lived on was not good enough for a patient. He was more relieved because he found Ralph in very good spirits.

"Ha! Russell, you are back already. You surely heard my announcement."

Puzzled at the two faces looking at him, Ralph continued. "Please sit down. This is Elise. She is a nurse in the hospital. She has been taking good care of me. If not for her, I do not think I could have survived. I would have died of hunger and loneliness. Elise, this is my bosom friend Russell. I preferred to come see him first as soon as I arrived in Cameroon. You can imagine what is between us for me to do so. I spent a wonderful week with him before he left for Yaounde three days ago. I'm sure he's left his mission in Yaounde unaccomplished just to rush back and see how his poor friend is."

"What happened?" Russell asked impatiently. All the introductions were not important to him at that moment. Ralph was brief in his narration, which he shared between gulps of delicious pepper soup.

In fact Elise had taken it as a responsibility to see that Ralph ate well since the afternoon she had bought food from the roadside and watched him grimace as he tried to get something into his stomach. He had explained that the food tasted delicious but the fact that it had been bought from a strange woman selling by the roadside had given the food a different taste. All efforts to convince him had failed. Her decision to feed him had stemmed from an attraction, which she could not explain. She felt drawn to him and wanted to keep him happy. This was not from any duty consciousness, but from something deeper. She felt at ease with him and enjoyed his jokes. Their two-day acquaintance was enough for them to realize that there was something more between them. She enjoyed the way Ralph ate the food she prepared. Just watching him eat was a pleasure.

"Why don't you join your friend?" Elise asked Russell. She stood up to dish some pepper soup for him.

"From a lady like you I cannot refuse." Elise felt flattered and smiled. After dishing for him, she excused herself, giving them the opportunity to discuss all they needed to discuss.

As soon as she was outside Russell exclaimed, "F.G.! You have to keep that name. You remember what we used to call you at the university. Fast Guy! Now just tell me how it all happened. I sure didn't expect to see you so well taken care of."

"I have told you all. She took pity on me and decided to feed me. I did not ask for it. She is a nice girl and I like her for what she is." After a pause he continued. "She is a beautiful woman. Real African beauty!"

While Russell was getting to know more about Elise, she was getting some raillery from her colleagues at the nurse's station. She was not on duty that morning but since she had come to give breakfast to Ralph she decided to go and greet them. They had noticed Elise's attachment to the patient and wanted to tease her.

"How is your husband today?" One of the nurses asked.

"Is he my husband?" she asked. Then she realized this was going to lead to an argument in which she could not defend herself. She changed the topic.

"You are the nurses on duty. So you should know more about his health than me." She had made up her mind not to be

19

offended by such remarks. The nurses were not through with her yet.

"What did you bring for him this morning? As I was passing by the door just now, I smelled something delicious."

"You should have gone in to see for yourself." Elise answered with a smile as she made to walk away.

"Elise! Elise!" The other nurse called her back.

"Please tell me. How can you take such good care of a total stranger?"

"Put yourself in his place. Would you have been happy if you were neglected in such circumstances?"

"No, but does he augment for you to prepare the food you bring to him everyday?" the nurse pursued.

"Chei! These women! Can't you sacrifice for somebody in need?" Elise exclaimed. She was becoming exasperated by these questions. With a smile she excused herself and went out.

At the door of Ralph's room she heard Ralph asking, "Did you by any chance see my mother in Yaounde?"

She knocked and went in. She wanted to hear about his mother. She was curious about his background but hadn't the courage to ask, for her first attempt had not been successful.

"You told me she'd moved to a bigger house in Elig Essono, but I was waiting for you in Yaounde for us to go there before this prevented you from coming."

Elise's hopes of hearing more about the mother of this remarkable man crumbled.

"Then I will give you her telephone number so you can call her. I am sure the phone in this hospital does not work. You will have to do it from your office."

While this conversation was going on Elise was putting her plates and dishes into her bag. The food was all eaten and she felt happy. Even Russell had looked contented as he wiped his hands and mouth. Russell was a handsome man in his own way. He was dark in complexion, but not as dark as Elise. Her heart glowed with pride at the fact that these two men liked and appreciated her. At the door, she turned to look back, and found both men smiling at her. Ralph winked at her and her heart missed a beat.

It was the fifth day of Ralph's stay in the hospital and his mother had not yet come. His mother could not have heard of his state and not rush over immediately. When Russell phoned, he had been told that she had gone out. Further inquiry did not bear any fruit since Russell's knowledge of French was limited. However he managed to get the message across that Ralph had been involved in an accident and was in the Bamenda Provincial Hospital. Ralph could have felt like an orphan abandoned to the care of other people. But he did not. Elise's good food, constant care and interesting character, combined with Russell's companionship and the attention lavished on him by the nurses in the ward kept him from feeling moody. He enjoyed bantering with the nurses, for he had a good sense of humour. The nurses had given him the name "Guy" as a compliment and everybody else was using it as if it was his name. When Russell had heard it he had roared with laughter, for it was not much different from the one they had given him in school.

"Guy, you have found a real mother here," sister Pamela remarked one morning when she came and found Elise's basket still waiting to be collected. "I hope you did not charm her."

"Oh sure I did. When I first set eyes on her I stated chanting a spell."

"I hope you are not going to carry her away with your spell, for she is one of our best nurses."

"Your spell has to be stronger than mine to be able to keep her here. I will not leave this hospital without her." With this statement they both started laughing.

Listening to the footsteps of the nurses and to those of Elise in particular had become a game, and each passing day increased his proficiency in identifying them. Each time he heard Elise's footsteps he waited for her to appear with a beating heart. The best days were when she was not on duty. She would spend hours with him, listening to his stories about life in France. Russell also spent more time with Ralph than in his house. He took his meals there. Elise's behaviour towards the two men was really motherly. She encouraged them to eat, especially Ralph who she said needed more food than drugs. Whenever the three of them were together, the atmosphere was one of relaxed familiarity. Russell never ceased to marvel at the

21

effect Elise had on his friend. At her appearance, Ralph would break into a broad smile. He also marvelled at Elise's ability to behave towards them as if she had known them all her life.

Elise enjoyed when Ralph kissed her palm as if she were a queen. She loved the feel of his palm on her cheek, the soothing caress on her arm and the secret smiles they shared. In Russell's presence whenever Ralph displayed such intimacies, she would look at him like a mother admonishing a naughty child. She did not like such displays in the presence of anybody. Ralph in his turn allowed no lengthy discussion with Russell about her. His respect for her neared adoration.

Elise on her part loved Ralph deeper than she could admit even to herself. She had fallen in love with him the first day she saw him. Her interest in him was more than the maternal instinct. She had never felt towards a man like this. She had a settled mind now. There were three other men interested in her, but at the age of twenty-three, she thought it was time to start looking for a husband rather than jumping from one man to another. This desire was pushed to the bottom of her heart lest her interest be misunderstood. Though she loved Ralph, she had no designs on him. She thought he was far out of her reach. Moreover she so far knew very little about him. She was happy in his company and that was enough for now. She would have liked to handle the situation alone but her limited income could not suffice. She had taken the decision to save the sum of twenty-five thousand francs every month after paying her rent, and nothing could make her change her mind. She had very little money left and she did not want the quality of the food she prepared for him to reduce. She was in a fix and did not know what to do. But she kept all these worries to herself. How her colleagues would laugh at her if they knew.

The next afternoon after eating the rice and stew she had brought, Ralph looked at her pensive face and asked, "Elise what is worrying you? You know that I do not like to see you without a smile on your face."

Elise did not realize that thinking about what she was going to cook for his supper had contorted her face.

"It is nothing. I was just thinking."

"Yes you were thinking. I could see that, but about what?"

"It is nothing of importance."

"But I would like to know," Ralph insisted.

"It is all right, Ralph. It is not important and I see no reason why I should tell you. It is over." She smiled and Ralph was satisfied. She did not want to stay long that afternoon and started packing the dishes as soon as he finished. But Ralph stopped her. Then held her hand and asked her to come and sit by him on the bed.

"Elise, you know that I like you." Elise was secretly pleased to hear this but kept her face impassive. He continued.

"I appreciate all you have been doing for me. You are really God sent. Whatever I give you is nothing compared to what you have been doing for me. Money cannot pay for what you have done." He sent his hand under his pillow and pulled out an envelope, which he handed over to her. Inside was the sum of thirty thousand francs. When she saw it, she did not know how to react. She was so relieved that tears almost came to her eyes. Ralph noticed this and did not understand why she looked so sad. He was confused and asked.

"Have I said or done anything to hurt you? Please tell me so that I should not do or say it again."

"Thank you, Ralph, Thank you very much. You have done nothing to upset me."

With this she got up to take her bag, wished him goodbye and walked out without looking behind.

Elise had always avoided cleaning the wound on Ralph's leg where the plaster of Paris had been cut off for easy treatment. She allowed her partner to do it. But this morning she had no choice. Her partner had not yet arrived and it was a quarter to eight already. She wondered what must have happened to make Sister Pamela so late. She had never been absent from work or come late without a good reason. There must be something seriously wrong Elise thought. She went ahead to administer drugs to the other patients with the hope that by the time she got to Ralph's ward Sister Pamela would have come. At nine o'clock, Sister Pamela was not yet at the

23

hospital so she steeled herself to face the ordeal. It was an ordeal because she had watched him wince with pain when the wound was being cleaned and did not want to be the one to inflict the slightest pain on him. Elise reluctantly pushed the trolley towards Ralph's room. Her greeting was brief and she set to work.

She gently brought her hand to the gauze that had been pushed into the wound to absorb the pus. The wound was healing beautifully and there was not much pus so the gauze was stuck on the wound. She soaked the wound with spirit and gently pulled out the gauze. She used more spirit to clean the wound. While she applied some penicillin ointment and closed the wound Ralph looked at her face and his thoughts were far away. If ever he wanted a wife then Elise stood a good chance. Which woman could do so much for a stranger? He wondered. She must have a heart of gold, he concluded. He thought of the other girlfriends he had had. They had not been like Elise. He had found her philosophy of life quite interesting. She believed that you got from life what you put into it. She was so simple and so unaffected. You could see through her. But how far Ralph could see through her was still to be determined.

Ralph had a knack for perfection. He had time and time again tried to suppress this tendency but it surfaced when he least expected it. Each time he found he had offended someone because he had expected more than the person could offer, he covered up with his sense of humour. He did not like to hurt people's feelings if he could help it. A healthy relationship was what he cherished most. He was friendly with all the nurses who worked in the New Private ward and they had developed a fondness for him. The first room they visited when they took over duty was always Ralph's. It seemed they needed his infectious smile to keep them in the right mood to withstand the innate dispositions of the other patients made unbearable by the sense of helplessness. He complimented them on their attire.

"You look smart this morning, sister," he would say to one of them.

"Your uniform is stainless white sister. It is enough to drive away all the microbes in this ward." He would say to another. After listening to the footsteps of yet another he would say to her as she came into his room, "Sister, your steps are so brisk. They are the footsteps of the conscientious nurse who is always prompt wherever she is needed." The nurses loved this and their smiles and thank yous made him forget his troubles.

All his life he had never understood the vital role the medical corps in general and nurses in particular played in the continuous existence of humankind. All he could remember was when he was taken to the hospital at the age of five or six. At the sight of the syringe he had screamed. The nurse threatened that if he moved while he was being injected, the needle would break in his buttocks and they would have to be operated for the needle to be taken out. He had hated her and consequently anybody in white overalls was his enemy. During the years of his youth he had not given them a thought. He was a healthy young man and looked at nursing as on of those duties performed to earn a salary. Living day-to-day with nurses now, he got to appreciate their work and the fact that it was a job that needed precision and perfection and compassion. There was no allowance for negligence or even a mistake. Not to talk of uncleanness or sluggishness, for this would cost the life of a patient.

Ralph had developed one of the habits bred of inactivity and being on the same spot for long. He mentally checked each nurse as she attended to him. He checked caps, shoes, uniforms, fingernails and even breath. Elise tried to keep to the medical ethics as far as these points were concerned. But this morning things were not the same. She had been in the hospital until late the previous evening keeping Ralph company. The thought of washing and ironing her cap before leaving her room that evening had completely escaped her mind. The next day she discovered to her dismay that her three caps were all dirty. She took a sheet of typing paper, folded it into the required shape and pinned it on her head. Unfortunately for her she had to clean Ralph's wound that morning. As she bent over the leg, the sharp edges of the cap attracted his attention. No cloth could have such sharp edges.

"Why are you putting on a paper cap?" he asked as he stretched his hand to touch it. The pin holding it in place was loose and the cap fell off.

"I am sorry," Ralph said when he noticed the mortification on her face. She had to leave what she was doing to pick the cap up and pin it back. When she started to dress the wound again, her hand was trembling. She bit her lip and tried to keep tears from coming. Ralph noticed this and did not understand what was happening. He tried to make as if nothing was the matter. But the conversation was one-sided. Elise could not trust her voice to speak. What was there to say? She could stand criticism from anybody, not Ralph. She had displayed gross inefficiency and a carefree attitude towards her job. Her usually conscientious nature had been made keener by her desire to impress Ralph and to show him that she was a good nurse. But it now seemed as if all her efforts had been in vain. She succeeded in controlling her emotions and after packing the instruments on the tray she managed a smile and excused herself.

"I am sorry Elise," Ralph repeated as she wheeled the trolley out. He could not understand why she had taken the incident so badly. Throughout the morning shift she avoided his room. This left him miserable. At midday she came to check on his medication.

"What is the problem Elise? You do not look yourself today. You know I always like to see that smile of yours." Elise did not know what to say. She could not tell a lie that she was not feeling fine, for this would only provoke more questions which she would only answer by telling more lies. She did not want to be caught in a tangle of lies. Moreover, she could not put into words what was actually worrying her. After reflecting, she herself could not understand what was eating deep into her. She felt sort of betrayed but was aware at the same time that the picture she had been trying to create had not been blotched anywhere. This was the first time she had really felt ashamed in front of Ralph.

Many other nurses used paper caps and many had had theirs pushed off and had just laughed over it. Was this the way she was going to react if someone she loved annoyed her? She wondered. If that were the case, then that love would not last. As she filled in the report of their shift of work, she thought over the events of the morning and made up her mind to forgive

Ralph for what he had done. She could not bear to be away from him.

Ralph was not aware of the extent to which she was suffering emotionally. After handing over duty at two thirty, she went to Ralph's room only to tell him that she would come to see him in the evening. The smile was back on her face.

"Please raise my pillow a bit higher," Ralph requested. As she bent over him to adjust the pillow he pulled her to himself and kissed her right on the lips. She could not resist him for his arms held her firmly. This was his first open display of his affection and she was taken aback by its suddenness. It did not last long enough to give Ralph the satisfaction he expected. Elise was breathless as she drew away. She could not believe what was happening. Her heart was thumping wildly. She quickly turned to look at the door to make sure nobody had been a witness of what had happened. The door was ajar but fortunately there was no one in view.

At the moment of contact with Ralph, all her senses were numb except the feel of his lips on hers and his arms round her. When he let go, he looked at her face to see her reaction. She looked both pleased and scared. Scared of what? He could not tell. Ralph knew that this was not the first time she had been kissed, but when something you had been expecting takes you unawares, it can be a bit frightening.

"I will come in the evening," she repeated as if he had not heard her when she first said it. As she walked home, her body ached for Ralph's touch and her head ached from the emotional turmoil of the morning.

Lying on her bed after eating, she turned on her radio and allowed herself to be lured to sleep by the rhythmical drone of the announcer's voice. It was time for the Luncheon Date announcements with announcements from the South West Province. She had not fallen deeply asleep when this announcement came to her ears as if from a distance.

"Ma Pauline Ngode of Great Soppo Buea requests the niece, Miss Elise Ebende of The Provincial Hospital Bamenda to urgently come to Buea for a matter that concerns her."

Elise quickly got up from the bed wondering whether she had really heard her name. At that moment there was a

27

knock on her door. Her neighbour had heard the announcement too and had come to inform her.

"Did you hear the announcement?" the lady asked.

"It's just two weeks ago that I received a letter from her. What must have happened?" Elise asked herself aloud. The lady was one of the nurses working in the same building with Elise but not in the same ward. She advised her to leave immediately.

"Tomorrow is your day off and it is Saturday. If you leave this evening you will be able to come back on Sunday morning to begin night duty. So you will not even be absent."

Elise's mind was aboil with conjecture as she packed a few dresses into her travelling bag. She had not even eaten. She hurriedly boiled some water and made some garri. While she was eating she remembered that in her absence, Ralph would have no food in the evening. She put some rice on the fire and went to take a bath.

Although Ralph had a radio by his bedside he was fast asleep at the time of the announcement and was still asleep when he felt a touch on his arm. He was surprised to see Elise earlier than he expected.

"I have to travel this afternoon. My aunt in Buea has made an announcement calling for me. So I am leaving." Ralph was speechless. It was so sudden. Although Elise had brought him some food he knew he was going to sleep without eating. How was he going to eat without Elise? She had become an integral part of his life in the hospital and he could not bear her absence. Elise continued, for she had seen the anguish in his eyes.

"I hope Russell will come and keep you company. I will be back on Sunday morning. I will take the night bus so I'll be able to rest before I come to work on Sunday night. Stay well." She turned to go.

"Elise." She came back. He removed his wallet from under his pillow, pulled out a ten thousand francs note and gave it to her.

"Have a safe journey." He held her hand and did not want to let go. She gently detached her hand and went out without another word.

3

lise arrived in Buea at midnight. When she knocked at the door, only Aunt Pauline got up to welcome her. Elise was too tired to ask any questions. In her room she quickly fell into an exhausted sleep. She stirred at the sound of a voice near her. It was Saturday morning and her aunt had gone to the Soppo Market and the children could not resist sneaking into her room to wake her up. At the moment of waking, she remembered why she had come to Buea. Her aunt was still at the market so she did not need to worry herself unnecessarily. She allowed herself to enjoy the presence of the children. They cVictoriad on the bed and got under the blanket. She felt snug in their presence and this gave her a sense of belonging. They were telling her stories and fighting to sleep next to her. The bed sheets were all rumpled and half of the blanket was on the floor. She surveyed all of these and was happy to be back home again. The simple abandon with which the children played made her wish to be a child again.

The rhythmical ringing of a bell could be heard in the distance. It was gradually coming nearer. The voices accompanying the bell could now be heard. With the shifting attention typical of children, they all abandoned her and rushed outside to see what was happening, leaving Elise alone in the room with all the disorder around her. She was undecided whether to go out and join the children watch what was happening or stay behind and tidy the room. The pull to be a child again and watch the scene with them was stronger. As a child she had always admired these women in their choir gowns singing and waving white handkerchiefs as they matched pass. Her aunt was with them but not dressed like them. She was at the tail end of the line. When they got to her door, she waved to them promising to join them soon. They were the women of the

29

Christian Women Fellowship going to sing at the occasion marking the celebration of the African Day of the Child.

"Elise my daughter, how did you sleep?" She embraced Elise as if she had just arrived. The children were around them, not wanting to miss the fun of the reunion.

"Deborah, today is Saturday. Remember the work you have to do." She admonished her first daughter who had become the eldest since Elise's departure for training at the Bamenda Training School for nurses and her employment at the hospital. She was a form four student at the Bilingual Grammar School in Molyko but had not yet realized that her mother expected her to be her next in command at home. As soon as you have given every child food, make sure that they wash their uniforms, socks and pants. I do not need to remind you of this every weekend."

The purpose of these instructions was also to get the children occupied and not give them the chance to listen to what they were going to discuss. She always avoided the situation where children listened to adult conversation. Aunt Pauline got Elise into her room. She was so excited with the information she carried that she could wait no more. There was also no need to keep Elise in suspense. Elise was also big enough to be told the truth about her parents.

"Elise, I am happy you heard my announcement and came immediately. What I am going to tell you is of great importance. You are a woman now living your own life. I brought you up as my child and I am very concerned about your happiness. I have never hidden anything from you. Have I?"

"No, aunty," Elise responded. Her head was bowed and she was tracing the lines on her palm. Her aunt had always talked to her this way when there was something serious. The last two times had been when she had to leave home for the first time to go to Bamenda for her training where she would have to live far away from all the people she knew. The second had been when her aunt had asked her if she had a boyfriend. She had been embarrassed but that had given her the opportunity to ask questions that had been bothering her. Her aunt's responses had helped her a lot. Now she waited patiently for the bomb that was going to change her life.

"Do you remember that I once told you that your father was in America?" Aunt Pauline began. "Well, we never wanted to have anything to do with him or his family, considering what happened to your mother."

Elise's heart was thumping now. She had never really believed what her aunt had told her. If she really had a father, why had he never bothered to find out about her? In her childhood she had always admired and even envied children with their parents in church or at end-of-year graduation ceremonies. But that was long ago. How was she going to react to a father now?

"He could have at least asked about me," Elise replied after a long silence.

"Let us not go into that. The blow was too much for the family to bear. We did that in your interest. We have brought you up with our meagre resources and now you are earning a living. If we have not given you what you expected, we could not have done better."

Elise loved her aunt very much and never wanted to hurt her unnecessarily. But the issue of her father was a sore spot. She would have loved to know more about him but there was no one to tell her. She had once heard two women wondering why her aunt was suffering for her when her father was a rich man in America. Each time she succeeded in forgetting about his existence, something cropped up to remind her of him.

"I am grateful aunty for all you have done for me," Elise murmured.

"Now listen," Aunt Pauline continued. "Your father loved your mother very much. For what I know, he was good to her and cannot be blamed for what happened. There are many people who come here from America. I have heard that your father never got married again and has no other child. Makia, the son of Aunty Enanga up in Bokwango, has come back from America and brought me this letter from your father. I do not know how he got to know, but I am sure they must have talked about your mother."

"May I see the letter?" There was a tremor in her voice and her hands trembled as she took it. She read through the letter. The first part was addressed to the family begging and

31

explaining how he had battled with his family to get them to contact the grandparents of his child to no avail. He wrote that he knew that they would never forgive him for what had happened but they must understand that his intentions were genuine and how he too has suffered, having taken the vow never to marry again.

The second part was addressed to Elise. It had the tone of a man in dire need of being accepted. He blamed himself for neglecting her, begged her to accept him, and promised to make amends for the lost years. By the time she got to the end of the letter, her eyes were flooded with tears and she allowed them to flow over onto the letter. Her Aunt watched. She pitied this child who had grown up like an orphan but at the same time with the knowledge that there was a father somewhere. She wondered the cause of the tears. Was it happiness at the thought that at last a father existed and cared, or sorrow over the loss of a mother Or was it pity for this man who had lived all his life with a ghost and was now calling desperately on her to bring some meaning into his life? Sobs raked through her body as if they would never stop. Her aunt held her close but said nothing. There was nothing worth saying. Words have no meaning in such situations. She let her cry. Crying was a good tranquilizer. What would she have said to the child? A child? No, a woman who would have to make her own decisions.

"Do you feel better now?" Aunt Pauline asked when the sobs subsided. "I cannot say anything. You have to decide for yourself," she concluded.

The rest of the day was too long. Elise lay on her bed and thought of her life. Her childhood days always had a shadow at the edges. In her moments of intense joy, there had always been a void. In her teenage years, the desire to fend for herself had pushed her from secondary school into a professional school. Now two people had suddenly imposed their existence. First there was Ralph who had made a deep impression on the sands of her life. She had felt she would be standing on solid ground if she had someone like Ralph to love her. Now her father whom she had never seen was supplicating her acceptance. What was she to do? Was she to gamble on an unknown father or ignore him and continue her relationship with Ralph?

32

At her departure for Bamenda that evening, she told her aunt she was confused and would write later to tell her what she had decided to do. This was just stalling for time, for she needed a father in her life. But what was she going to do about her relationship with Ralph?

Elise always dreamt about her mother and the picture was always blurred. She had never succeeded in putting together the whole story from the bits and pieces she had gathered from conversations and gossips she had overheard. This is what had happened.

Some twenty years ago, before Elise was born, Andre met and fell in love with Anne. Anne was a grade two teacher at the Government Primary School in Tiko. Andre was a worker at one of the parastatals in Douala. Anne was of average height with a chocolate colour enhanced by the moist humid climate of the coastal regions. She was a rare beauty that eluded description. Despite her beauty, she was a humble and responsible woman. Although men were drawn to Anne like butterflies to a flower, she did not take advantage to exploit them. She had been in and out of love a number of times. She had always broken off the relationship whenever she noticed that the men were not serious and just wanted fun. She did not expect these early relationships to blossom into marriage, but she expected some responsible behaviour from the men. She did not cherish the situation where a man would want to possess her body and soul when there was no life commitment between them. She spoke less when she was in the company of men and appeared shy and fragile. This was a quality that made men be inquisitive about her. She lived with a nephew, Lawrence, who attended the school where she taught.

She had met Andre while she was travelling on a bus from Yaounde to Douala on the Guarantee Bus Service. They were fellow passengers. Andre had been watching her as she conversed with the friend whom she had come to visit and who had come to the bus stop to see her off. As he observed her he told himself that this was the type of woman he would like to know. He had managed to get a vantage position on the bus so that the last person to come in would have no choice but to sit by him. Anne was the last person to come in so she sat by him. As soon as the bus took off, she withdrew into herself. It is very easy to get into a conversation in a bus and Andre looked for an excuse to talk with her. He noticed that she was holding a newspaper in her hand.

"May I have a look at your paper, please?" She handed it over to him. It was *The Cameroon Tribune*. He flipped through the paper, reading the headlines. On page five were two cartoons of a man working in a garden. The first cartoon was complete but the second had eight parts missing. The game was to compare the two pictures and locate the missing parts on the second cartoon.

"You look bored. Why don't we play this game? It will take off the strain of the journey."

She looked at his face and he gave her an encouraging smile.

"All right," she replied. "Will you begin?"

"Yes, I will, but we have to put some rules. Can we say each person has five seconds to find a missing part on the second cartoon?"

"All right, you still have to begin. I will keep the time." After five seconds Anne said, "Time out. Have you found any?"

"Not yet," Andre replied. "Now it is your turn. I will keep the time." After five seconds he whispered in her ear, "Time out, have you seen any?"

"Two."

You are quite observant," he remarked. "Here is a pen. Mark them."

When Andre had first looked at the cartoons he had seen one missing spot but he had not wanted to be the first to score a point, so he had allowed her the opportunity. As they continued to play the game Anne was loosening up and he liked this very much.

They were engrossed in looking for the missing parts on the second cartoon when their bus slowed down and their ears were assailed by the sound of wailing. The bus stopped and they got out. In front of them were four other vehicles, but after that was a scene that made their blood run cold. A tipper carrying sand had collided with a bus carrying nineteen people.

34

The tipper had tumbled by the roadside spilling the sand it carried. The bus was somewhere in the bush and they could hear people shouting for help. More vehicles had stopped on the other side of the road and two of the occupants of the bus were being brought from the bush to the roadside. They were both mutilated beyond recognition. At the sight of this, Anne felt her legs go weak under her. Fortunately, Andre was holding her hand. He now had to hold her close to prevent her from falling. He led her away from the sight back to the bus. To do this he had to send his arm round her waist. As she recovered from the shock of what she had witnessed, she started responding to his soothing words.

"Please, do not cry. That is the fate of man. We cannot understand it as we cannot understand many other things."

"Not this way, not this way," she sobbed. I would not like to die this way, mutilated beyond recognition. Let me die quietly in my bed."

"We cannot choose how to die neither can we choose our parents," Andre consoled her. He held her close and in her sorrow she unconsciously pressed closer to him. She was happy that he was there to give her moral and physical support. It is this display of feminine weakness that brings out the best in a man and Andre was not different. He did all he could to console her and show that he cared.

When the bus took off again, there was silence as each person contemplated what they had seen. No matter what the religions of the world may say, death is a rotten and terrifying thing. No matter the manner in which it comes, it does not change its very nature. Talking soon resumed. Passengers commented on the accident and tried to determine who was at fault. Anne did not utter a word. Neither did Andre who had been deeply shocked by the blood-soaked bodies, which had nauseated him. He had felt like vomiting, but he had had to behave like a man for Anne's sake. Now he was occupied by something else, for life denies death and asserts itself. His thoughts were on the woman who was sitting by his side, whose hand he was holding and whose body was pressed to his. He would have liked to know where she lived and worked for he was bent on continuing this relationship. But there was no way he could find out because of the state in which she was.

When they arrived in Douala, he used the opportunity of getting a taxi for her to know where she lived.

"In which neighbourhood do you live? I want to see you safely in a taxi before I go away."

"I do not live here. I live in Tiko."

"In Tiko? I thought that you live here in Douala. What do you do in Tiko?"

"I am a teacher in the Government Primary School." At that moment a taxi slowed down beside them and she asked if the taxi driver could take her to the South West bus stop in Bonaberi. This assured Andre that she had told him the truth. He stood and waved as the taxi drove away.

Wednesday was the worst day for Anne. Apart from doing her normal duties as a classroom teacher, the headmaster had assigned her the task of collecting fees. At the end of each week, she calculated what had been paid and handed it in with the list of pupils and their various classes. Wednesday was the day she did her calculations because her class usually went for Domestic Science after break. She was sitting in her empty classroom involved in this task when she heard somebody asking for her from the teacher next door. Before she could go out to see who the person was, they were already at her door.

"Hello Anne, I knew I would meet you here." Anne was stunned and could not respond immediately. "Are you not happy to see me?" Andre asked in the ensuing silence. Anne realized that her colleague was still there looking at her. She had to act fast not to give him any ideas.

"Andre, what are you doing here?" she exclaimed with delighted surprise.

"I have come to see you."

"You are not serious. I am sure that you were just passing, and since this school is by the roadside, you decided to stop by."

"No," Andre insisted. "I came to see you." Her colleague turned and walked back into his classroom. He had heard enough. Anne led Andre into her classroom.

"Please sit down." She offered him the only seat fit for an adult, which was her own chair.

"No, just sit where you were sitting. I do not mind sitting on one of these benches. It will make me feel like a schoolboy again and I will not mind your being my teacher." They burst into laughter. Work was over for Anne. There was no way she could concentrate now that Andre was with her. While Andre looked around the classroom marvelling at the fact that he had actually passed through this stage too, Anne was packing the lists into her bag. Fortunately she had counted and put all the money into her bag before Andre's arrival.

"Let's go home. You will be more comfortable there." Andre could barely manage to squeeze his long legs out of the narrow space between the desktop and the bench. Her house was not far from the school. If she were alone with the amount of money she carried, she would have taken a taxi, but now she preferred moving on foot. The time taken to walk home would give her time to check her bearings as far as Andre was concerned. Her response to his visit would depend on what they discussed on the way and his response to her questions. They left the school compound and were some distance away when neither of them had spoken. The situation was becoming uncomfortable.

"Don't you want to talk to me Anne?" Andre asked.

"I haven't gotten over the surprise of your visit yet."

"So you do not yet believe that I can come to visit you?"

"Exactly. I did not expect to see you again."

"Did you wish to see me again? Are you happy that I have come?"

"Why do you ask such questions Andre? You can see for yourself that I am very happy to see you."

"After we separated in Douala last week did you think about me?" Andre asked. He was probing and digging into her heart. Anne had not stopped thinking about him when she came back. She always hoped to see him again. But now that he had come, she did not know what to say. She turned his question to him.

"Did you think of me when you left?"

"My presence here is enough evidence of that. Since we met in the bus, I have not stopped thinking of you. If I did not come here today to see you I do not think that I would have been able to do anything else."

When they entered her house he stopped for a moment to look around him. Her parlour was well kept. The chairs looked as if nobody ever sat on them. The floor was very clean. Everything was where it was supposed to be. His eyes eventually came to rest on a picture of Anne hanging on the wall. There is nothing as unreliable as the human countenance. No expression can be kept for more than a few seconds. The photographer had clicked his camera at the right moment. Her face looked serious, but with that touch of a smile on her lips, which were full and made more sensuous by the lip gloss. Her eyes looked challenging yet alluring. It was at this picture that Andre was gazing as if in a trance, when Anne came out of her bedroom where she had gone to keep her handbag and take off her shoes.

"Why don't you sit down?" Anne asked. He turned away from the picture and without sitting down looked at her. They looked at each other.

"Andre, you are making me nervous."

"You shouldn't be. I was just wondering what you were thinking about when that picture was taken." This sounded so ridiculous that she smiled.

"I am sure that you must be hungry. I still have to get something cooked. Just keep yourself busy with these pictures."

Andre did not know anybody in the pictures in the picture album. But each time he came across a picture of her, he would look at it as if he wanted to get it printed in his mind.

While they were eating, her nephew, Lawrence, came back from school, greeted them and went into his room to remove his uniform. As he passed through the parlour, he had just enough time to look at their guest. In his room he could not resist having another look at him. He had never seen such a handsome man before. Andre had a very dark complexion with milk white teeth. His angular face and his sideburns made him look like a film star he had seen in a magazine. After some time he pulled aside the curtain to have another look. Andre had seen the curtain move and understood the inquisitiveness of children. As the boy passed to go and meet his aunt in the kitchen he smiled at Andre. Andre returned the smile.

"Whom are you smiling with?" Anne asked.

"You have a smart young man here."

"Oh, Lawrence, he is a good boy. I do not know what I could have done without him."

Andre and Anne spent the rest of the afternoon talking about a number of things. Andre tried to gear the conversation towards getting her to talk about herself. Anne did not want to say anything about herself, which the situation did not warrant. She brought in an anecdote each time the conversation verged on lagging. They were mostly stories about happenings in a primary school. Andre admired her presence of mind and her ability to evade questions she did not want to answer. They spent the afternoon thus engaged without noticing the passing of time. It was five thirty when Andre looked at his watch.

"Oh. How time flies. I must be getting back. How does your weekend look?" Andre asked.

"I have nothing in particular planned."

"Then I will come up and we will have a nice weekend together. Agreed?"

"It's all right with me if you have that much time to spare."

After a vehicle from Victoria picked him up, Anne strolled pensively back to her house. She mentally checked through all his words and actions to see if any of them bore any resemblance to pretence. She was sure that he was interested in her. What she had to determine was whether she was interested in him. There was no doubt about this but she was not spared the uncertainty that characterizes a budding relationship.

"Aunty, who is that man?" Lawrence asked as soon as she got back to the house.

"He is a friend I met when I was coming back from Yaounde."

"Aunty, I like him."

This statement coming from Lawrence took her unawares. She had always told him the truth when he asked questions which she thought he should begin to understand. She had also made him feel free to express his opinion when he was asked. But for him to have expressed his opinion about a complete stranger unasked was beyond her.

"Do you?" she asked.

"Yes, aunty, I like the way he talks and smiles."

Anne looked at the child again wondering what was wrong with him. He had never reacted this way to the few men who visited her. He had always greeted them with an impassive face and responded sullenly when scolded for his attitude. He had accepted their gifts with a polite thank you.

Saturday morning was cold and wet, a real damper. Anne had slept with a fluttering in her stomach, caused by the anticipation of what was going to happen the next day. She did not know what to expect. While waiting she occupied herself with doing her laundry and cleaning her floor. Lawrence did not hurry over his chores. He too was waiting. He washed his uniforms and cleaned the kitchen shelves and floor. At ten am the rain ceased and the sun came out with such suddenness that it burnt the skin. Just about this time, Andre arrived. His shoes were so muddy that the doormat could not be used. Anne had to bring him a pair of her slippers to wear before entering the house. His feet were bigger than hers but fortunately it was the all sex type of slippers so he could manage. While he was changing into the slippers, Lawrence had taken his bag into the house. He returned to take his shoes and clean them. He was excited.

"So how are you this morning?" Andre asked Anne as he sat down.

In response Anne said, "I hope you had an enjoyable journey back to Douala."

"When I left Douala, it was raining cats and dogs. I am surprised to find sunshine here." Lawrence had been listening to what Andre was saying and the expression cats and dogs made him begin to imagine how the two animals made rain to fall. He memorized the phrase planning to ask Andre later what it meant. Anne wondered the direction towards which this conversation was drifting. No one had answered the other's question.

40

"We are not staying here today. I want us to go somewhere. So whatever you have to do, do it quickly and let us go before the rain begins again." He had not given Anne the chance to ask any questions or say something that would jeopardize what he had planned for the day. She was grateful for this because she did not want to be left in suspense or be forced to ask what they were going to do. The prospect of staying at home and talking as they had done the previous time was not appealing. Lawrence brought back his shoes already cleaned and polished again. Andre took up his bag and brought out a ball and a packet of biscuits and gave them to him.

"Thank you uncle. Thank you very much."

Anne was in the kitchen. When she heard this, she came out to see what was happening. There was Lawrence with the biggest smile she had ever seen him produce and clutching a new ball. What a thoughtful man Anne mused. Then aloud she said, "You really know how to get to children."

"You just need to put yourself in their place and you would have no problem relating with them." He turned to Lawrence who was still admiring his ball.

"Won't you go out and play with your friends?"

"I will uncle. But I want to stay with you first. You are all alone in the parlour.

"All right. You are my friend. So you can stay."

Andre asked him about his activities in school and their conversation soon turned to football. From the excitement in his voice, Andre knew that with the new ball, Lawrence was going to be the hero among his friends. This was a big improvement on the old smelly one made from unprocessed rubber. The child expressed some very technical ideas in football. Andre was surprised that a small boy could know so much. But Lawrence was just being the typical Cameroonian with football running in his veins. Through the conversations Lawrence expressed his gratitude at being given a new ball. It was not just the fact that he loved having a new ball that made him so happy. It was more the fact that it was from Uncle Andre.

By midday, Anne and Andre were in Victoria. He took her to the Atlantic Beach Hotel where they had a delicious meal of fresh fish in tomato sauce and rice. When lunch was over,

41

they strolled hand in hand under the trees, appreciating together the beauty of nature. She marvelled at the incomprehensibility of it. Shrubs, trees, and flowers lived in harmony while human beings with highly developed brains lived in such discord. The sun was hot overheard but underneath the trees it was cool and refreshing as the sea breeze rustled the leaves. Under a tree Andre turned her to face him. He looked deep into her eyes. With his forefinger he traced from her forehead to the tip of her nose. By the time his fingers got to her nose, his lips were on hers. All along he looked into her eyes. They did not waver. She had been expecting this to happen and the moment he turned her to face him, her pulse rate had increased. There was a throbbing sensation in her loins as she raised her lips to meet his. This was harmony. Andre was gentle as he caressed her back though his body cried out to be fulfilled.

At 4 pm they went down to the beach market and watched the fishermen rowing in and later haggling with the market women over prices. They sat on an abandoned boat and watched what was going on around them. Andre felt so relaxed. He thought that if his life could continue this way, the restlessness that he felt would gradually disappear.

It was getting dark when they left the beach. They got a taxi for Tiko. On the way Anne wondered what she was going to do when they arrived in Tiko. She had never allowed any man to sleep in her house. What would Lawrence think of her? She had never given her neighbours fodder to feed their wagging tongues. But what was she going to do? How was she going to send him off to Douala just like that, after what had happened in the Botanic Gardens? Her worries kept her silent and the excuse of being tired served the purpose.

Andre in his turn was also wondering what was going to happen. He did not want to go back to Douala to spend the night alone in his bed after what he had experienced with Anne. He knew he was not going to sleep. He wanted to spend the night with her but was not certain on how she was going to react. Although she had allowed him to kiss her, and it was evident that she was willing and had also enjoyed the kiss he had this feeling that he had to tread with caution. Anne looked at his profile and the serious look on his face gave the impression that he was angry. In fact, it was just the tension in his mind preparing to absorb whatever disappointment awaited him. Anne would have given anything in the world to know what he was thinking at that moment. She realized that seventy-five percent of the decision lay in her hands. The school compound rushed by and she quickly made up her mind. They were approaching the entrance to her house and she could not allow him to go alone.

"You look so tired. I hope we will stop at the house first," she ventured.

"Well, it all depends on you. But I would like to rest first before going back to Douala."

Both of them had been avoiding mentioning the idea of his going back that night. As they moved hand in hand to the house, Anne did not want the silence to extend else in the house the situation would be awkward.

"It has been a wonderful day Andre. I loved every moment of it. I really enjoy your company. I hope we will have more of such times again in the future."

At the sound of approaching footsteps, Lawrence opened the door.

"Aunty Ele…" He stopped when he saw Andre. "Uncle welcome," he said in an uncertain voice. He smiled at him and took his bag. He did not know where to keep his bag. He looked at his aunt to answer the question on his face but she was looking elsewhere. So he kept it on one of the chairs and took his aunt's bag into the room. Anne quickly changed her dress and went into the kitchen. The situation was worse now that Andre was right in the house. There was no way out. How was she going to invite him into her room? What was Lawrence going to think? She put some of the *quacoco* her mother had sent on the fire to warm while she went to take a bath. As she was bathing, she caught snatches of what Andre and Lawrence were saying. "…if she would allow me to sleep here."

"But you cannot travel in the night to Douala. It is too dangerous." The noise from the shower stopped as Anne tried to hear more. The conversation also stopped. When she came out to the parlour again, Andre was still where she had left him.

"Please aunty, will you allow uncle to sleep here?" Lawrence asked with all the innocence of a nine-year-old boy. The plea in his eyes amused Anne. The child was not aware of the load he had lifted off her mind.

"If he wants to, he is welcome." She looked at Andre and there was this mischievous smile on his face.

"He can sleep on my bed," Lawrence announced.

"The bed will be too small for the two of you," Anne insisted.

"Then I will sleep on the chair in the parlour."

"Lawrence, you are a very clever boy. You are my very good friend," Andre said as he stroked Lawrence's head. "I will not allow my friend to sleep on the chair because of me." He turned to Anne.

"You do not want me to see what is in that room of yours?" He turned to Lawrence. "Is there anything in there which she does not want me to see?"

Lawrence was enjoying the attention he was receiving. His aunt's room was not out of bounds for him so he could not understand why someone like Andre, such a nice man, could not enter there.

"So can I go and have a bath?" This question was addressed to Lawrence not to Anne. He shook his head in affirmation. To enter the bathroom Andre had to pass through the bedroom. Lawrence realized the enormity of what he had done. He looked at his aunt to see her reaction. She had been listening to them with a smile on her face. Lawrence took this as acceptance of what he had done.

While Andre bathed, Anne dished out the food to put on the table. Lawrence helped her place the plates. He did not need to ask before setting the place for three people.

Andre, with one of Anne's loincloths round his waist and his singlet looked at the food on the table.

"It smells so delicious. When did you prepare it?"

"It is a surprise too. My mother sent it from Victoria. She sends me raw food and sometimes cooked food. But I was not expecting this. My cousin must have brought it. She lives in Tiko town."

"Maybe she knows that I am here. That is why she sent it."

"She does not even know you Andre."

"Very soon she will know me."

While they were eating she saw the gleam in his eyes and thought how disappointed he could have been if she had allowed him to return to Douala. Anne felt at ease. The thought of what her neighbours would say receded into the background. She was not going to care about what they say. She was grateful that Lawrence had taken to Andre and they were already friends. She remembered how Lawrence had told one of the men who was pursuing her that she was not in the house when in actual fact she was in her room. This had saved her from an unpleasant visitor.

They were too tired from the day's activities, especially Lawrence who had been playing all day with his friends. The new ball had given them more impetus to resist tiredness.

Lawrence had fallen asleep on the chair on which he was sitting and had to be led to his room. Back in her room Anne's body tingled with expectation as she changed into her nightdress. She made sure that she did not reveal any part of her body as she dressed. Andre pretended to be reading a magazine, which he had picked up at the bedside. All his senses were alert, waiting for the moment when she would come to the bed. When she turned round, Andre got up, lifted her off her feet and carried her like a baby to the bed. He laid her down so gently that she did not know when her back touched the bed and his lips were on hers. It was a moment of complete giving as he hugged her close to him and she clung to him. Andre did not rush. He used all the skills in his experience to get her ready. When he was finally led into her planet, it was full of exploding stars. It was such a wonderful sensation that both of them wished it would last forever. The journey on the planet did not cover miles but the energy used was much and they were approaching the summit. When the biggest star exploded there was oblivion. If death were like this then many people would like to die many times. As he held her after in his arms, Andre let his mind wander wonderingly.

Exhausted and contented, they fell asleep in each other's arms. To Anne, this was the essence of life. Andre was so strong, so exciting and an expert. Andre too had been surprised at her reactions. Her usually calm attitude belied an inner sensitivity. The night was so short and soon it was dawn. Anne woke up with the feel of Andre's arms around her.

It was a Sunday morning. She could have slept in, but she was used to getting up at six o'clock. When she tried to get up, Andre pulled her back.

"Don't go away my darling," he murmured in his sleep. She lay back and when she was sure he was fast asleep again, she gently got up. Lawrence had gone to sleep without seeing them together in the same bed and she did not want him to find them in bed. She kept herself busy in the kitchen waiting for Lawrence to get up. At the sound of movement in the kitchen Lawrence got up and came over.

"Good morning aunty. Can I go in and say good morning to uncle?"

"No. He is still sleeping. When he gets up and comes out, you are going to say good morning to him."

Anne was so preoccupied with what this child thought about her that she did not want him to be witness of the fact that they had slept together. She did not understand why she was ready to ignore what the neighbours thought of her, but not what this child thought.

"Have you brushed your teeth? You better hurry and take your bath. Breakfast will soon be ready. Remember that you have to take some flowers to Sister Grace, to decorate the church."

When Lawrence was eating, he asked, "Aunty, are you not coming to church today?"

"You know that uncle is still here and has to go back to Douala today."

"But he can come with us to church before he goes."

"He is still sleeping. Before he gets up, baths and eats, it will already be late."

Andre was listening to this and was glad that he was going to spend some time alone with Anne before he left.

46

"I want to see uncle before he leaves. Will he wait for me?"

"Of course he will. Now get your shoes while I go and cut the flowers for Sister Grace."

As soon as Lawrence left the house Anne went and met Andre on the bed. This time the journey was gradual, allowing them to savour with pleasure the sensations that coursed through their bodies.

Andre left at 11 am, as soon as Lawrence came back from church. As he sat in the bus heading for Douala, he made up his mind to see this relationship to the end. Since there was no telephone in the school where Anne taught, he contented himself with weekends. The weekdays passed quickly as each weekend kept him in anticipation.

The following weekend, he took her to Douala. It was while they were conversing in his parlour that Andre realized the similarities in their names.

"Do you realize that our names sound the same?" he asked.

"You are so imaginative, Andre. Can you combine them?"

"Aned is a good one. How do you like it?" Anne thought for some time.

"It is all right but I do not think I would like to call you that, though it is a sort of combination of our names To me it does not really carry the weight of what I think we feel for each other."

"So what do you suggest?"

"I do not have anything to suggest. But I think the way you will call me or I will call you will depend on the situation."

"You sound so unromantic, Anne. I would like to have a name to call you to show my love for you."

"You can call me honey, sugar, love, anything that comes into your mind."

"You sound so matter of fact. You don't seem to take what I have said seriously."

"Andre, what matters to me is the fact that you love me and I love you. Names do not matter with me. When I am angry with you, do you think I will call you honey? Honey is sweet but anger is bitter."

"Why should you be ever angry with me Anne?"

"Those are the ups and downs in life that make it interesting."

"I will never give you the opportunity to be angry with me. I promise."

He held her and kissed her before she could say anything.

Three months later, they paid a visit to her parents. There was nothing intended in the visit. They just wanted to see how her parents were going to react to her bringing a man to see them. Lawrence came along with them. The visit was brief and they left Lawrence to spend the weekend. Anne had just introduced Andre as a friend. But her mother had looked at him with hope. She did not miss the glint in their eyes when they looked at each other. She had looked closely at him as mother with marriageable daughters usually do. Andre had assured her in his heart that Anne was the woman for him. The mother got to know about Andre from Lawrence who in his childlike enthusiasms could not stop talking about him. The mother concluded that for a child to like an adult in that way for no good reason, there must be something good in the man. This relationship went on for six months when one day Andre decided to break the ice. They were lying in bed during one of her visits to Douala.

"Anne, we have been together for all these months. I do not want it to end this way. From the first day I saw you at the bus stop in Yaounde, I knew that you were the woman for me. But I did not want to rush anything. I wanted us to give ourselves time. I want to marry you Anne. Would you accept me as a husband?"

Anne had been thinking along such lines too. She had not even confided her wish to her mother. Now she wondered how they were going to react to this news. She looked at him straight in the eyes. What she saw there was enough to give her the courage to stay by Andre, no matter what happened. She buried her face in his chest. He sent his arms round her. With his masculine strength, he almost squeezed the breath out of her.

There was no need for words. This love blossomed into a child who one day would be left on the high seas of life struggling to find love, the type of love that existed between her mother and father.

4

"Ralph, how can I make you understand what I am saying? Don't you realize the risk you are taking? You cannot blame me for not coming earlier."

"Please mother, I have said that I want to stay here and get well. I am well taken care of. You do not need to worry."

"Ralph, my son, you surprise me. You have been in France all these years and seen the advances made in medical science. CUSS is the best in Cameroon and you turn it down to stay in this insignificant hospital? Do not blame me if anything goes wrong."

"Mother, I know how I feel. If I were not getting better, I would have come with you immediately."

"Russell, please talk to your friend. I do not know what is wrong with him."

But what could Russell say? He understood why his friend was obstinate.

Madam Perpetua Essin had arrived Bamenda that Sunday morning with the intention of whisking her son off to Yaounde without delay. All the arrangements had been made for him to be admitted at the University Teaching Hospital in Yaounde. Although it was a weekend, she was determined to leave the next day for Yaounde. She had come with the image of the boy who had left for France five years ago in mind. She did not know that she was going to meet a man who could stand up to her. It was evening already and this was her second attempt to convince her son to go back with her. After her appeal to Russell, there was an uncomfortable silence. This was broken by a knock on the door. It opened slowly and Elise looked in to see if Ralph was asleep. She had this impression because the room was so quiet. Instead, three pairs of eyes turned towards her. A dazzling smile immediately broke over Ralph's face. Madam Essin fixed her eyes on Elise. Elise was not yet in her uniform so

50

Madam Essin thought she was a visitor. But the smile on Ralph's face made her to believe that she was not an ordinary visitor. "Elise, you are welcome back. How was your journey? How is your aunt?" He did not give her the chance to answer these questions but went ahead to introduce his mother. Elise was dying to look at her but the intensity of her gaze made her look away each time their gaze met. When Madam Essin turned to speak to Russell, Elise took a good look at her. Mother and son were not alike except in such similarities that manifest themselves only to closer observation.

"I think we should go home. You have been here since you arrived. I think you should go home eat and have a rest," suggested Russell, easing the electric tension that was building up again. When Elise had come in she had unconsciously gone to sit near Ralph on the bed and he had taken her hand in his. This had confirmed Madam Essin's suspicion and put her in a different trend of thought as she left with Russell.

Madam Essin was a lady in her early fifties with a well-preserved figure and a husky voice. She moved with an expert femininity, a calculated fluidity of flesh that suggested availability but was totally respectable. Her going out seemed to have left more breathing space in the room. The room was not stuffy, but her presence did not call for free expression. As soon as she was outside, Elise turned to Ralph to answer the unasked questions in her eyes. Instead he pulled her to him and kissed her on her cheek. The past two days had been dreary and his mother's persistence to take him away had kept him very uncomfortable. Elise's presence was a balm on his mood. He wanted his mother to see her for him to gauge her reaction. The kiss on Elise's cheek did not change her unease. He looked closely at her. The smile he expected to see was non-existent. She looked worried.

"Elise, you look tired, but tell me about your journey. What was the problem that your aunt wanted you so urgently?"

"It was nothing serious. She was just making a fuss over nothing. She had some information which she wanted to tell me in person." Elise did not say anything more. She was interested in what had happened in her absence especially as his mother

51

had come. She continued, "I am sure you will leave tomorrow or the next day since your mother has come."

"In fact, we were talking about it when you came in. My mother still thinks I am a small boy. She wants to take me back to Yaounde. But I do not want to go. I am being treated like a king here. Moreover, I do not want to leave you and the care you are giving me."

She was happy with the part that concerned her but her professional ethics called her to order.

"Why did you refuse? You will have more advanced treatment in CUSS than we can give you here." It was Ralph's turn to be hurt.

"So you don't want me to stay here?"

"No, that is not the point. I just want you to have the best treatment."

"There is no other treatment better than the one I am receiving here. I know that the attention I receive from the nurses is not given to other patients the same way. Don't you think I love and appreciate that?"

"Oh, Ralph. You have always been so understanding." It was her turn to give him a kiss on his cheek, which he would have preferred on the lips.

"How have you been since I left?" She took his file and looked at the entries. He had been in hospital now for twelve days and had to start practicing how to walk with crutches.

Madam Essin had a sleepless night as she tossed on Russell's bed. It was a strange bed in a strange room in a strange town. She was disturbed not only by the strangeness of the situation but also by the thoughts that coursed through her mind. This was not the son she had held close to her breasts at the airport five years ago. How he had changed! He had grown into a handsome man in his late twenties. He had come back with a Masters Degree in Accountancy. She was very proud of him. But his refusal to come with her to Yaounde where he would be better taken care of was beyond her comprehension. Maybe that woman had something to do with it, she thought. She had been startled by her resemblance to her cousin Andre, but thought no more of it. She had not missed the smile and the change in mood in her son when she had arrived.

Madam Essin was a businesswoman. Business was her life wire and she did not want to miss any opportunity that looked profitable. She turned her thoughts from her son to think of the items she would have to buy at the Bamenda Market to sell in Yaounde. She had heard that foodstuff was very cheap in Bamenda and in her mind she mentally ticked off those she wanted to buy. At the same time she was determined to take her son back with her to Yaounde. While she would be convincing and breaking his resistance she would be doing some buying as well. She was good at shooting two birds with one stone. With this settled in her mind she dozed off into a deep sleep as the day dawned.

It was nine thirty the next morning when Madam Essin arrived at the hospital. It was Ralph's first day on his feet since he had the accident. He had to start learning to move with crutches. The plaster was still on and this impeded his movements. When he had completely brought his weight on his legs, he felt a momentary uneasiness as if he was going to fall. He gradually allowed his weight to bear on the leg. Even with this he needed support. Since the other nurses were busy with other patients, Elise offered to help him exercise along the corridor. As they moved up and down the corridor, Ralph did not feel the heaviness on his leg because his mind was elsewhere. As they proceeded gradually to the end of the corridor Madam Essin appeared at the other end and stood watching them. They were talking as they walked slowly and at one point they started laughing. The sound of Ralph's laughter had made Madam Essin stop. Elise had heard approaching footsteps but did not look round because many people came to the wards in the morning. Then she had the feeling that someone was watching them. She looked back and saw Madam Essin. She was glaring at them. She whispered to Ralph.

"Your mother." They did not get to the end of the corridor but turned slowly round with Elise keeping step with the patient.

"Hi! Good morning, mother," Ralph began. He could not continue because of the look on his mother's face. Her brows were wrinkled and there was all evidence that she was not pleased at what she was seeing. This expression soon disappeared. She recognized the fact that her attitude would only antagonize her son.

"Good morning, Ralph. I can see you are really getting better." There were smiles on her face now, but Elise and Ralph did not miss the frown. She continued, "I am really happy to see you so well taken care of." She did not acknowledge Elise's presence. Her emotion when she had looked at her son lying there helpless had been pity. This had changed to anger at the independence he had displayed. Today she felt jealous because she could have been the one helping Ralph to walk, not that woman who seemed to have a grip on him. She was angry at the fact that this woman meant more to her son than she did.

"I hope you slept well mother, after the strain of the journey yesterday," Ralph continued. He was his old self again and kissed his mother affectionately. Elise could not believe that he was the same Ralph who had avoided looking at his mother for fear her countenance might make him change his resolve. After settling him in bed Elise excused herself and went out. The problem that had brought Madam Essin to Bamenda had not yet been solved and she had to be diplomatic about it.

"I admire the way the nurses work here," she began and glanced round appreciatively, then continued, "especially the one who just left us. She looks like a good girl."

"She is the one who has been helping me all along. If not for her, I do not know what I would have done."

"I am so sorry I could not be here…"

"Oh, mother, don't begin that again. She is an angel. But I am not angry with you."

"I know you're not. But you must have felt disappointed when there was no response to your radio message and telephone calls. If I were in your position, I would have felt the same. Now that I am here, I'll try to do my best."

The bullying and mother-knows-best attitude of the previous day was no longer there.

"I am your mother and the sacrifices I can make for you, no other person can," She continued. The expression on Ralph's face changed. She noticed this and surged ahead to get what she thought out of her heart.

"It seems as if you love that girl. But I am sure that it will pass. I know that you are too sensible to get involved at this stage." Ralph looked at his mother and restrained himself from saying what was on his mind. He knew his mother well. She was easily overtaken by surprises, but if she knew about anything beforehand, her barricade would be insurmountable.

"I can't help liking her mother, after all she has done for me. You want me to be an ingrate? Now I am trying to move about. It will not be long before I will be able to move on my own. Then I will come to Yaounde and do nothing but eat and sleep and you will then do all the fussing you want."

Madam Essin was making no headway. Her anger was rising again.

"Ralph, I know that you want to stay here because of that girl. You would be a fool to fall in love with a girl like that. This is the time to be serious and get married, not to be falling in and out of love like a teenager. I would not even consider her as a daughter-in-law."

"All I have said is that I like her mother. Have I talked of marriage?"

In the silence that ensured, Madam Essin assessed the situation. She had enough experience to know when two people are in love. Elise had been polite to her but not as she would have been if she did not assume some relationship. The stony silence and Ralph's firmly closed lips were obvious signs. He did not want to look at her in the face. She resorted to the ultimate approach. She left her seat to come and sit on the bed by his side. She took his hand in hers and held it as she spoke.

"Ralph, you know that you are my only child and my life is centred on you. I don't need to remind you of this fact. Do I? What do you want me to do? Do you want me to leave you here and return to Yaounde? Does that mean that if I were sick somewhere and you came to take me away and I refused you would leave me and go away?"

"Yes, mother, I would leave you if you gave me convincing reasons for wanting to stay."

"So what are your convincing reasons for wanting to stay?"

Ralph was trapped. He did not want to go into details about his relationship with Elise so he did not answer. The mother continued.

"You know that I live on the business I do. I have already ordered fresh tomatoes, okra and beans to take to Yaounde and sell to retailers. I have paid already. If you insist on staying I will stay with you and lose all that money. Where will I even stay? I cannot stay with your friend and inconvenience him the way I am already doing. If you want to place me in this difficult situation, go ahead." His mother continued with a hint of resignation in her voice. Ralph looked at her and realized she was getting old. She was no longer as young as she was when he had left for further studies. Under stress, in spite of the foundation cream and make-up, nature had still asserted itself. His defence was breaking. He looked at her profile and saw lines of age and resignation. He felt sorry for her and his resolve was softened. He saw no reason in making her suffer now. He would let her have her way. After all he had his own mind.

A week later, Ralph was lying on a sofa in his mother's parlour in her Elig-Essono residence. A sentimental record was playing on the stereo. It was 11 am and the house was quiet. His mother had done everything to keep him comfortable even to the extent of increasing the house help's salary from twenty to thirty thousand francs so he could spend the whole day in the house with Ralph attending to his needs. Before he used to do his chores and go away. She did not fail to tell some of the girls she considered suitable for him to come and visit him and keep him company. Some were girls he had known before going to France. His mother introduced those he did not know. At times they were children of her friends or just her small friends as she called them. Ralph used to wonder how his mother came to make friends with women far younger than she.

This morning, as if on a wisp of cloud, he was back in Bamenda. As he lay on the sofa half asleep, he recalled in his mind's eye the events of his last hours in Bamenda. When he had told Elise about his decision to go back to Yaounde with his mother, she had sat quietly. Ralph had looked at her face trying to read what was on her mind at that moment. For as Shakespeare says, a man's mind is like a book. She was looking down at her legs so he could not look into her eyes to read what was there. In her eyes her emotions were battling with each other. In the confusion they spilled over.

"Don't cry, Elise. I am not going away forever. I will come back for you, my love. Please try to understand. My mother won't leave without me. I am going just to satisfy her."

Elise wiped her eyes and swallowed a lump that was building in her throat. At that moment it seemed to Elise that her world was at a standstill. Ralph's going away was like stepping from firm ground onto quicksand. Her uncertainty was enough to drown her. She got hold of herself and lifted her eyes to look at him. In her eyes he could see the deep loss and emptiness that could not be put into words. The feeling of loneliness was already creeping over him but he reassured himself of the decision he had taken.

As he reclined on the sofa, he imagined what she was doing at that moment. The picture that came to his mind was her face with a smile displaying her evenly set white teeth and the dimple on her cheek. The picture stayed on his mind as if it was a pause on a TV screen. He basked with pleasure and a smile came to his lips. These were the types of memories that made him happy in spite of the inconveniences and frustrations imposed by his immobility. He was dozing with this smile on his lips when the opening of the door made him get up with a start. He had not heard the knock.

"Good morning, Ralph. You look radiant this morning with that smile on your lips even in sleep." He had been caught unawares but was pleased that she had come, so the smile stayed in place.

"Claudette, it is so nice of you to think that I need company, especially at this time of the day when everybody is at work. Please sit down." Instead of sitting on another chair, she came and sat by him on the sofa.

"Sam! Sam!" Ralph called. "Have you got something for us to drink?"

"Let me have a look." Sam called back as he wiped his hands with a napkin at the kitchen door.

"No beer for me," Claudette said as she settled herself more comfortably. Ralph's plastered leg was on the other side so he had to move his good leg to make more space for her.

"Sam, you do not need to look in the fridge. Bring us the brandy from the cupboard and two glasses. Also bring us a bottle of Fanta."

To Ralph, Sam was not house help as such. He looked on him as good company. Sam was older than Ralph and wiser in the ways of the world than he was. Sam was not bad looking at all. He was smart, neat and used his initiative. The difference between the two of them was not so much their ages as their educational backgrounds. Ralph felt at ease with him and was even tempted to share some secrets with him. He considered it too early to get Sam into his confidence though he appreciated his honest approach to life. When the drinks arrived, Ralph wanted to be the gentleman but his reclining position could not permit him.

"I am not a stranger in this house, Ralph. Let me serve myself." Claudette poured some brandy until the glass was almost half full. When she lifted up the bottle to pour Ralph's share, he declined explaining that he was on antibiotics and was discouraged from taking alcohol. She poured some Fanta for him.

"For your quick recovery," she said and took the glass to her lips. When she put it down it was half gone. Ralph had watched warily as she poured the drink, and now he was taken aback by the amount remaining.

Claudette was a constant visitor at the house since Ralph's arrival. She had come to the University of Yaounde when Ralph was doing his last year. They had lived together in the same mini-cite. Before his departure for France, he had got to know her but not particularly. Her previous visits had always been in the evenings when there were many people around. Now was the ideal time to know how life was treating her.

"You have not changed much Claudette. But you have filled out well and there is all evidence that life is treating you well." A cloud passed over her face, which she quickly dismissed.

"Well, I cannot really say so. But I am surviving. At least I have a job."

The cloud was as a result of her dissatisfaction with her present situation. She had not achieved what she had dreamt of achieving academically. She had hoped to go for further studies but she had ended up working in a drab office, not earning enough money and still single. They talked about many things and people especially the few acquaintances both of them knew. From their conversation it was evident that life treated people differently. Some were so successful that their social positions were enviable. For the girls she had known, many of them were married and in Europe or living a plush life in Yaounde. Some of those not yet married had pushed themselves up the administrative or social ladder.

"Tell me Claudette, are you still waiting for the golden prince?" He asked as he lifted her left hand to look at her finger. He asked this in such a joking manner that he was not prepared for the melancholia that clouded her face. But she did not allow this to linger.

"Ralph, I am not getting younger. But I do not want to rush into any relationship that looks potentially catastrophic."

"What do you mean by that?" Ralph asked." How can you know a situation that is potentially catastrophic?"

"Ralph, you have been out of the country for some time. Things have changed. Just keep your eyes and ears open."

This statement had intrigued Ralph. During this conversation Claudette's buttocks had come into close contact with Ralph's good leg. She leaned backwards a bit to allow maximum contact. This contact had generated some warmth in her and she took advantage of the situation to occasionally caress his leg. She would in a mood of pretentious absentmindedness stroke his good leg as she spoke.

"Claudette, I did not want to pry, but you have said something very illuminating." They were silent for a while. Claudette contemplated the statement she had made and wondered whether she had said more than she should have. She was not making much progress and was afraid the situation might deteriorate.

"Ralph, I am afraid I should be going. I have stayed long enough. I do not want to tire you out."

"No Claudette, do not go. Since I came back, I have not had such company. Please stay a bit more. I am sorry if I said anything to annoy you." A smile resettled her in her seat and she poured herself another shot of brandy. After sipping it she seemed to regain herself. It was her turn to dig into what was on Ralph's mind.

"You have not said anything about the lucky girl. Is there one Ralph?"

The suddenness of the question surprised him because he was thinking along just those lines. He had the queer feeling that Claudette might have read his thoughts on his face and tried to hide his embarrassment.

"In fact, I have not yet given it a thought," he lied. "I still have to settle. And this (pointing to his leg) is not making it easy."

As he spoke she was looking at him. She winked at him then said, "Ralph you are quite a handsome man. Has any woman ever told you that?" To concretize her statement, she lowered herself and kissed him on his cheek. Her breath reeking with brandy filled Ralph's face and he held his breath and tried to smile at the same time. He was enjoying this bit of flirtation but was not carried away. She seemed to know the wiles and ways of the fair sex and applied them with charm and facility.

"I never knew you could be so charming. I wish I had got to know you earlier."

"But it is not yet late. You know what? I always had the feeling right when we were at the university that you never noticed me. And even if you did…" She stopped as if she was no longer sure of what she was about to say.

"Please continue. I really want to know what you thought of me." She hesitated before continuing. "I was not good enough for you."

Ralph burst out laughing and she joined him.

"I thought that you were going to say something awful about me. I hope you didn't see me as conceited, because I wasn't. I was like any other boy. I played the game too." They burst out laughing again.

"And when will the game end?" she asked.

"Does it really end?" there was more laughter. Then she continued. "Oh Ralph, you are not so naïve after all. It seems the tendency is innate in men and it surfaces at the appropriate circumstances."

"So you want to say that all men are like that?" he queried.

"There are exceptions but these are rare. Women are more resistant than men."

Ralph did not want to make a response to this last statement. He preferred to keep his opinion to himself.

"I hope you will stay for lunch. It will soon be midday and mother will join us. You can imagine the way she fusses over me as if I were a child."

"You cannot blame her, Ralph. Her life is centred on you."

"You sound like her. She has her life to live and I have mine. We are two individuals."

"But you cannot refuse the fact that you bring immense joy into her life."

To this Ralph again made no comment. He imagined what she would have done if he had died in the accident.

"She is so proud of you," Claudette continued. "You need to know how she talks about you."

Ralph began to wonder where all this was leading. He didn't like allusions to how his mother treated him. To get away from this trend of conversation Ralph called out, "Sam! Sam! What are we having for lunch?"

"Your favourite, sir." Sam never addressed him as "sir" and he wondered why he did then and made a mental note to ask him later. Footsteps outside prevented him from asking what his favourite dish was. He parted the blinds to see his mother coming. He braced himself and silently prayed for her to skip the display of motherly affection. He could stand it without an audience. But please God, not now.

"I see you have company," remarked his mother as she came in. "So how is the leg today?" Instead of coming towards him she dropped her bag on the seat opposite them.

"Claudette has been keeping me company since morning."

"That's good,." remarked his mother.

"She has made the morning pass so quickly," Ralph added. Then he changed the topic. "How was business today? You look worn out."

Ralph had come to understand that his mother was happy when he showed interest in her and her affairs. He never missed an opportunity to make her know that he cared for her.

Since her husband had gone overseas and the trickle of letters had stopped, Madam Essin had taken her life into her hands. The education and the upbringing of her only child had so obsessed her that she had not committed herself into another marriage. Moreover, she had not married at the age that gave her another chance. He admired her determination to be a successful woman.

As she told them of her business exploits of the morning, he noticed an undertone of excitement. What could be responsible? He wondered. During lunch, Claudette was attentive to his every need and his mother kept up a lively banter. The meal was enjoyable not only because of Sam's expertise but also because of the company. Ralph's good mood particularly pleased his mother and she prayed for a miracle to happen. When Claudette finally had to leave, Madam Essin could not help commenting on the effect that her presence had on her son.

"You bring the best out of him, my daughter. I would be grateful for more of such visits."

Back in the house, Sam was carrying away the dishes from the dinning table. When he came to carry the two glasses from the sitting room, he lifted the bottle of brandy and squinted at the level of the liquid, shook his head and grunted. Ralph had been watching.

"What is that?" he asked.

"A sucker," Sam replied.

"What do you mean by that?"

"A woman consumes this quantity before midday? No..."

62

In a too obviously assumed gravity Ralph rebuked him. "Never talk about my visitors like that, Sam."

"Yes sir," Sam replied as he walked away with an ill concealed smile on his face. Although Ralph had to rebuke him for his comments, on further thoughts he found some truth in them. The quantity of brandy that Claudette had consumed was too much considering the time of the day. He knew that his mother was a schemer but there was no evidence to connect Claudette's visit and her actions with his mother. His mother came back into the parlour. She sat opposite him. He could imagine what she was going to say and decided to beat her to it.

"What do you think about Claudette, mother?"

"She is such a nice girl, so understanding and respectful. Imagine that she came and kept you company for so long."

"Why is she not at work today?" Ralph asked trying to show interest in her. In actual fact he was trying to see whether his mother had a hand in Claudette's visit.

"She is on leave and intends to stay a week in Yaounde before she goes to Douala."

"How come you know so much about her, mother?"

"She is like a daughter to me. Now why don't you go to your room and rest? Let me help you to your room." Ralph was really feeling sleepy but did not want to be led to his room like an invalid.

"I prefer to stay here, mother. I am putting on too much weight just eating and sleeping. I will read a bit then I will move out to the veranda."

"All right, I am in my room. I will rest a bit then I will go back to the shop. Remember to give me your prescription so I can buy the drugs before coming home in the evening."

"All right," Ralph replied as he searched for a magazine. Ten minutes later, he was asleep on the sofa.

Ralph's leg was healing beautifully though the plaster was a real handicap to his movements. His mother had succeeded in taking him away to Yaounde, but he had succeeded in convincing her to allow him to go back to Bamenda for the plaster to be removed. This could be done in Yaounde, but Ralph had other reasons for going back to

Bamenda. At that time his mother had not taken him serious. What was important to her was taking him back to Yaounde. She was sure that as soon as he got to Yaounde he was going to forget all about Elise. Ralph had to go back to Bamenda as they had agreed but when he brought up the subject his mother did not want to hear.

"Ralph, that plaster can be removed in any hospital. I have arranged for you to continue your treatment here. There are doctors here who can do your follow up."

"Do we have to argue about this again, mother? We agreed that I would go back to Bamenda for a check up and for the plaster to be removed. Why are you going back on your words? It will be six weeks next week. That is why I am reminding you." She stood and looked at him for some time.

"All right, please yourself." Madam Essin was finding it difficult to accommodate this new Ralph. She wondered how a son of hers could go against her wishes. She was the one who had single-handedly brought him up. She was his mother as well as his father. But Madam Essin had forgotten that he was a grown man. She had forgotten that he had stood on his own for five years without having to run to mama whenever he had problems. During five years, Ralph had grown out of the mould his mother had put him in during his childhood and early youth. Now as an adult she was trying to put him back into that mould. It was going to be a very tight and unpleasant squeeze.

In her shop that afternoon Madam Essin's mind was preoccupied. Why did her son always want to go against her wishes? She wondered. In her daydreams she had imagined a son who would rely on her and a daughter-in-law who would run to her for help. She assured herself that she would never allow Ralph out of her life. He had his own life to live but she was not going to bear being ignored or overlooked when important decisions concerning his life had to be taken. She counted on his being dependent on her. She thought of punishing him by abandoning him to his own means if he disobeyed her but gave up the thought as soon as it formed. How could she abandon him? She would die in the process. She then thought of the good times she had had with him before he went for further studies. She had basked in Ralph's successes in school. She remembered how she proudly stood by him for snapshots at his graduations and how she would discreetly leave the house when he came home with friends. With all these thoughts she decided that if he was going to Bamenda for the plaster to be removed, there was no problem. Then she recalled the nurse she had met at the Bamenda General Hospital. She wondered if Ralph's insistence on going to Bamenda was related to her. For a moment, she was ill at ease. No! He can only do that over my dead body! A mere nurse! Ralph should be wiser than that. A girl like Claudette was good for him. With a university degree they could go back to France if they wanted.

The afternoon was very boring as the flow of customers was at a lull. She was still preoccupied with her thoughts. She never liked a strained relationship in the house and was prepared to allow Ralph to have his way as long as he knew his limits.

5

ussell had been communicating with his friend and was waiting anxiously for his return. He had something to discuss with Ralph, which would put him in a better position to help. Since Elise's visit to Buea she had changed. Although she maintained her vivaciousness, there were times that he could read intense melancholia on her face. Her smooth complexion was creasing. He had tried to get her to tell him her problem to no avail. At first she had refused his invitation to a nightclub, or just an evening out. Maybe she thought he was going to act like the caretaker who takes over all caring. Russell was caught between and betwixt. His friend counted on him. How was he going to make this girl feel at ease with him without betraying his friend? He persisted in his visits to her house. When he noticed that she was beginning to resent his presence he came to a decision.

"Elise, I admire you. I like the way you behave. I know how you feel towards my friend and how he feels towards you. Ralph is my best friend. I cannot do anything to hurt him. Since he went away, you are not the same Elise I knew when he was here. He will soon be coming back. But I know that it is not his absence which is worrying you. In spite of all I have done to try to help you, you have resisted my help. I am giving you this advice as from one adult to another. You are not a child. If the change in you is due to his absence, though he has been writing to you, then as a woman, you still have a long way to go before you can cope with a man. If it is something else which you do not want to tell me, you will one day tell it to some other person. You are not an island. A problem shared, is a problem halved."

During this lecture, a transformation as well as a realization was taking place in her mind. Brooding over her problems did not take her one step towards solving them. Whatever was to become of her depended on her. She was the one to decide what to do with her life. She was not the only factor in her future happiness. Ralph was a necessary part of it. But what was really on his mind? She wondered whether Russell knew more than he was telling her. The knowledge that he would soon be coming eased her mind a bit. She decided to change her attitude towards Russell.

"I'm sorry I've been behaving like this towards you. I was a bit carried away by what my aunt told me when I went down to Buea. It was something in the family that I wanted to know. But it is all over now. Thank you for the advice."

The last statement was accompanied by a smile. Russell still had a feeling that there was something, which she did not want to tell him. After this they had become friendlier, but he noticed that the subject of her parentage was one she never liked to discuss. She only maintained that she was an orphan brought up by her aunt.

Russell knew when his friend would be arriving in Bamenda and if the bus was on time he would meet him at the stop. He left his office at two thirty but when he arrived at the bus stop, his friend had not yet arrived so he sat in a nearby bar and bought a bottle of beer to keep him company while he waited. The bar was full with drivers. It was their spot where they rested while their buses were being loaded. Here, one could hear all sorts of stories ranging from sexual exploits, to the characteristics of women, to money and the dishonest ways of getting it. In fact, they talked about all the situations they came across in the course of their daily activities. This afternoon they were engaged in recounting their proficiency in driving and arriving at their destinations in record time. Making maximum profit accompanied the satisfaction of being able to carry out this feat and recount it to an attentive audience. As Russell listened to these narratives, he never ceased to wonder at the outcome if there should be a headlong collision or if the vehicle should lose control. A rough looking dirty man was narrating how he escaped from custom officers from Idenau to Victoria through the CDC palm plantations, carrying three hundred litres of illegal petrol popularly called "funge." He was burly and busting with strength. He had thick eyebrows and thick

67

stranded eyelashes, under which bloodshot eyes rolled and sparkled as he recounted the exciting moments. His ill kept buns looked unhealthy as the hair curled over one another. It seemed as if his teeth had never seen a toothbrush as they merged with the black gums. As he spoke, specks of spittle flew from his mouth and Russell was happy he was not sitting near him. His shirt had contours of sweat at the armpits. The skin on his forefinger and middle finger was stained with nicotine. He spoke, smoked and drank at the same time. His whole appearance was so revolting that Russell could not bring himself to admire the feat of courage he was narrating or even smile at the humour in the narrative. This is what he told his audience.

He had been hired to go to Idenau and carry some illegal petrol. He left for Idenau at 4 pm with the hope of coming back when it was already dark. He hoped to slip through customs under the cover of darkness. When he reached the Customs checkpoint, he passed as if he did not see their signal to stop. About ten meters away from the checkpoint he slowed down as if he wanted to stop but only changed his gears and took off again. The Customs officers did not expect this move and were taken unawares. Before they could run to their vehicles to begin the chase, he had gained some distance on them. He left the main road and branched into a well known smugglers track in the palm plantations. The Customs officers knew that he was going to use this track so they followed him. Since he had the advantage of distance he again branched off where the palm trees were thick with undergrowth, stopped the vehicle and put off the lights. Soon he heard the roar of the custom vehicle. He saw the lights appear and pass. He waited for a while and started his vehicle. He retraced his path and came to a new one that had just been created but was not yet known by the Customs. The monotony of the palms as they swept past gave no room for landmarks. The only landmarks were rivers and small hamlets. The crisscrossing tracks were deceptive especially at night. The first village he came to passed in a flash. He did not bother to check where he was. He knew that he was on the new track. He only stopped at the second camp to ask. An instinctive foreboding that he had missed his way was nagging at his consciousness. He was in one of the camps which was far away from his intended route. The people of the camps were quite familiar with these tracks and guided him. He retraced his tracks. When he got back into the palms again, every place looked the same. He was confused and afraid. The petrol in his vehicle was running short. He had not anticipated that this was going to happen, so he had not carried along an extra gallon. It was getting to midnight when he could not still find his way out of the palms. To save petrol he had to park the vehicle and wait for the first streaks of daylight. It wasn't an easy wait as the minutes and hours crawled by. Anxiety and fear kept him awake most of the night.

The trip to Idenau was just a side activity from which he made some fast money because he was booked to drive a busload of passengers to Bamenda the next day. That morning it seemed as if his head was empty of sleep. At the Victoria bus stop he drank a bottle of Guinness and ate some kolanuts to help keep the sleep away. As Russell looked at him, he wondered why such an energetic man could not put his strength to better use than risking his life in such escapades.

Russell heard some shouting and looked up to see a coaster bus driving into the bus stop. It was from Yaounde and he knew that his friend had arrived. He did not wait to hear the end of the narrative. God is kind, he thought to himself as he left the bar. He could not imagine how the man would manage to drive to Bamenda the next day. By the time he got to the bus, Ralph was already out and looking anxiously for his friend. When they saw each other there were smiles of relief, and they embraced each other, with Russell taking care not to make his friend lose balance. Ralph in turn firmly planted his crutches into the ground to maintain his stability. In the taxi going home they talked on irrelevances although each of them was busting with information as well as questions. Once in the house there was no time to waste.

"How was the journey?" Russell asked.

"It was fine except for the fact that the bus made too many stops on the way, picking and dropping people. When we left Yaounde the bus was not full." Ralph was anxious to know what had happened in his absence. Instead of going straight to the point he started beating about the bush.

"So how is Bamenda?" he asked as if he was concerned about the welfare of the entire town. His friend knew what was actually on his mind, but he too parried.

"Things have been moving on fine. In the office there is not much work." He could not continue. The conversation sounded forced and he did not want to continue else he sound stupid or seem as if he were hiding something, so he went straight to what was on both their minds.

"Although I have not been busy this while, I have not been able to see Elise. I do not know whether there have been changes in the wards." Even with this statement, Ralph still asked.

"How is she?

"I have succeeded in breaking the ice, such a nice girl with so much on her mind," Russell commented. After listening to what Russell had to say Ralph's love for Elise was further strengthened by the desire to protect her. He wanted to be a mother and father to her. He wanted to bring joy into her life, that joy that only love can give. With these emotions ebbing and flowing in him he wanted to know more. He had made up his mind before he left Yaounde. Elise was the woman for him and he was going to do everything to get her. Ralph sat for a while in silence and Russell looked on, wondering what was going on in his friend's mind.

"Russell," Ralph began. "I want you to do me a favour. Promise me you will." With an incredulous smile on his face Russell wanted to ask his friend how he could promise to do something he had not been told yet, but kept his peace. Then a thought came into Ralph's mind. He was not sure yet how Elise was going to receive him. "Well, we will talk about it tomorrow," Ralph ended.

Elise had recovered from her worries and was going about the business of living. She had left the future to take care of itself. She was waiting to see what developments were going to take place as far as Ralph was concerned. She also waited to see what her father was going to do about the letter he had sent to her. Both were blind steps and if she did not take one, she had to take the other.

70

The afternoon that Ralph had arrived Bamenda, Elise was on the two to nine shift. Russell had gone to look for her at seven thirty. Her room was dark, the blinds drawn and the door locked. She was still at work. At nine thirty when she came back she was so tired that she just managed to eat something and climb into bed. At ten o'clock when Russell came to look for her again, her door was still locked and the blinds drawn. She was in bed fast asleep.

Since the plaster was still on Ralph's leg there was no question of their going out. So after eating some rice and soup, which Russell had prepared, they sat conversing and drinking what Russell had bought in the afternoon. There was beer for Russell and Coca Cola for Ralph. There was much to catch up on and the evening was not going to be boring but Elise's presence would have added more spice to it.

When Elise could not be traced, Ralph's doubts were further fanned. Although they had much to talk about, each time he remembered Elise there was a flutter in his heart. Russell noticed that his friend was not himself and knew the reason. Maybe talking about it would help.

"Do you know that when you left, Elise was avoiding me?" he began. Ralph just looked at him, not knowing what to say. Russell continued, "After all the time we spent together when you were hospitalized, I could not just make as if I did not know her. But it seemed as if she did not like my company anymore." Ralph was now wondering what could have sparked off this animosity. Maybe his friend was trying to step into his shoes. He looked at Russell straight into his eyes.

"You are my friend Ralph. I cannot be the one to come between you and Elise. If I do that then I am not your friend."

"Well, I was not thinking of that," Ralph began. "I had quite a different idea in mind," he lied. The he yawned voluntarily. He did not want the conversation to continue on this trend. Russell understood that he was tired.

"You must be very tired. Why don't you go to bed? I want to listen to the late night news before I sleep." He made to get up and assist his friend. But Ralph declined his help. Russell watched as he manoeuvred himself with his crutches into the bedroom.

Ralph's intense look when he had mentioned that Elise was avoiding him had shaken him a bit. The problem of getting a wife had been gnawing at him for a long time. There was this girl from the village whom his parents had wanted him to marry. She was a pretty girl but had just left primary school. This, coupled with the fact that there was no spark between them, had dismissed the whole issue. He momentarily winced at the insults his mother had thrown at him at the time. She had accused him of being the faggots that feed the lust of women who walk the streets.

He assessed himself and tried to imagine the type of girl who would make him a good wife. What came into his head were the normal things, which a man would expect of a woman. She should be educated and presentable. She should be able to bring forth children. She should be sociable and accommodating. A man should be able to go out with his wife and feel at ease in her presence. The woman should be able to contribute to the family income. These were recognized criteria. The thought of working class women who in the midst of a quarrel with their husbands would say "Without you I can still live" jarred him. But what is it that makes a good wife? This question can only be answered by living the experience. So where do I begin?" he asked himself. These thoughts had put him in such a daze that he did not know when the news ended. The closing tune of the radio startled him and he sat up. He sat thinking for a while and his thoughts now were all centred on Ralph and Elise.

Elise had sacrificed so much for a total stranger. Was that love? He wondered. He had watched the two of them together. They behaved as if they had known each other all their lives. Was that love? She seemed to have so much trust in Ralph. She had never discussed the contents of the letters, which Ralph had been sending to her. Even though she knew that he was Ralph's best friend she had never showed any sign that she expected their relationship to lead to marriage. Well, if this was love, then tomorrow was going to tell. He got up, changed into his pyjamas and got into bed, taking care not to disturb his friend.

The outpatient consultation was full with patients sitting on benches or standing. The hospital staff could be easily identified in their white overalls or white dresses. As Ralph waited his turn to enter the casualty section, nurses who had attended to him stopped to greet him and express their joy at seeing him looking so well. He was the centre of attention. One nurse, the elderly one who was with him in the reanimation ward on the first day, was so happy to see him that she begged the nurses in the casualty room to attend to him soon, saying he was an exemplary patient.

The machine for cutting the hard plaster was tested. It whirred and the blade made a buzzing sound. He winced as the appliance was brought near his leg. As the sharp blade chopped into the plaster, his heart kept missing a beat, waiting for when the blade would touch flesh, but it never did. The thick layer of plaster was soon peeled off revealing a layer of scaly skin with very little hair. He felt like scratching the whole leg but was prevented from doing so. The leg felt light as if it was not part of him. He had become used to the weight of the plaster for the six weeks that he had had it on. Now he had to start adjusting to his real weight. A liquid was used to wash the scales away and the leg looked healthy again although a little emaciated. The stitches were removed and he had to go back to the doctor for re-examination of the scar and bone. Although the bone had healed beautifully the wound was still tender. Some healing ointment was rubbed on it and it was covered with gauze and plaster before he left the hospital.

All along he looked at the ladies in white hoping to see Elise. Until he left the hospital, he did not see her and his uncertainty mounted. Even Russell could not understand why she was not in the hospital. He had barely prevented himself many times from asking one of the nurses who had worked with her in the ward while he was there. On their way home he wondered what he was going to do. He could not leave his friend and go to work without finding out where Elise was, because he knew what was on his friend's mind.

"Just make yourself comfortable. Sleep as much as you can. I will be back soon." With this he left his friend not giving him the chance to ask where he was going. A confused Ralph sat in the parlour while his thoughts whirled in bewilderment. He soon dozed off into a fitful sleep.

Monday was Elise's day off. What a way to begin the week! Her long sleep the previous night had been refreshing and she was full of energy to put her house in order. She washed her dirty dresses and hung them out to dry. She mopped the floor and was hanging out the rag to dry when she saw Russell coming towards her. She wondered why he was not at work. It was ten thirty in the morning, an unusual time for a civil servant to pay visits. How did he know she was at home? She wondered. If he had looked for her in the hospital then he had something important to tell her. The forerunner smile that precedes greetings was bright on Russell's face. She even noticed a twinkle in his eyes.

"What brings you here at this time of the day?" she asked. "I know you people don't have days off as we do." She kept up this stream of conversation as they moved towards the house. All along, Russell said nothing. He wanted to see her natural response to what he had come to tell her, so he took his time.

"Russell, you are making me nervous. Is there anything wrong?"

"No," he replied looking into her eyes. "Ralph wants to see you," he finally announced.

"Has he come? Where is he? How is his leg?" All these questions were asked in excitement and the twinkle in her eyes and the dimple on her cheek became more prominent.

"He is in my house waiting for you," Russell replied feeling a bit jealous. He did not want to stay around any longer.

"I should be going. I have not been at work since morning." He did not need to tell her that he had left Ralph all alone in the house. He knew she was not going to waste any time getting there. Elise realized she had displayed much emotion and tried to sober up.

"Thank you, for coming to tell me. I will go and see him after cooking." She tried to pretend indifference but it was too late.

"See you in the afternoon," Russell said as they shook hands at the door. Her heart was pounding wildly. What

74

cooking was she going to do when she had not seen Ralph? She was going to see him as soon as she had something decent on. After her bath she took care over her make-up. Although she never applied make-up flamboyantly, she knew just those shades of lipstick and powder that enhanced her natural endowments. Her plaited hair had lasted for too long and was in disarray. She undid it and, after combing it through, clasped it into a bun at the back of her neck. The pulling of the hair stretched the skin over her face making her cheekbones more prominent. It pulled on her eye muscles and gave her that fawnlike appearance that made her look so innocent. It was this look that men found so alluring. Each time she did her hair in that manner she felt more satisfied with the results than certain times she went to the hairdresser.

Even in an adult, some childish tricks still surge in the mind and the thought of springing a surprise on someone at times is irresistible. Elise had no doubts about how she would be received. If Ralph had sent for her, then he would be happy to see her. But she was sure he was not expecting to see her so soon from what she had learnt of what had happened the previous evening. Approaching Russell's door, she did not want her footsteps to prepare Ralph for her appearance. She wanted to witness his natural uninhibited response to her presence, so she made as little noise as possible. On the veranda, she went on tiptoes, knocked, opened the door and entered. The noise woke Ralph and he opened his eyes in surprise. He tried to stand thinking that the plaster was still on his leg. The sudden movement destabilized him and he lost his balance. Elise foresaw this and rushed to hold him. He clasped her in an unintentional embrace, which soon turned into a suffocating embrace while his lips searched hers. They pulled apart and looked at each other. Ralph pulled her to sit beside him. Words were not necessary to express their joy and relief at seeing each other again.

A deep exhaling of air said it all, but Elise could not leave it at that.

"I'm so happy to see you."

"Do you know that you have eyes like a doe?" Ralph asked in response. Elise did not know what a doe was but she knew Ralph had just paid her a compliment from the way he was looking at her.

"How is the leg? When was the plaster removed?"

"I was in the hospital this morning, but I didn't see you anywhere."

"Today is my day off, and I am here." He took her hand and held it in his, looking at her all the time. Elise felt a surge of excitement and uncertainty.

"How is your mother? She must have petted you well."

"She is fine. She is fine." The manner in which he answered made her submerge any further questions.

"Let us go to my place. I want to prepare you a good lunch." She stood up and tried to help him stand. He resisted her help.

"You can see for yourself that I do not need help. You can see the product of your labour." He made a show of moving elegantly to Elise's amusement.

Once they were in her house, he could not restrain himself. He held her and kissed her on the lips with his tongue parting hers. Choked by excitement, she broke off the embrace. But Ralph did not let go.

"I love you Elise. I have since the day I first saw you." This was beyond her wildest dreams. She was speechless. She turned away and walked into the kitchen. He followed and stood behind her as she stood and gazed through the window. When he turned her round there were tears in her eyes.

"Have I made you unhappy? If I have, then I am sorry. But I cannot hide how I feel. I love you Elise. Don't you love me?"

"I do. I do." Her voice was further muffled as he held her close against his chest.

"Then why are you crying? Please tell me why."

"I don't know why. I am so happy."

"I have not been flattering you Elise. I am serious about what I have said. It will not only remain at that."

"Please Ralph don't say anymore." She disentangled herself and half blind with tears she took a cluster of plantains and started peeling them. She wanted to be occupied to be able to control her emotions. She was also feeling hungry. Her

76

absence left Ralph uncertain as to what to do next. Ralph went to the parlour, sat down, took a deep breath and exhaled. He stared at his shoes with his mind in a blur. He listened to the sounds in the kitchen waiting for it to cease and for her to come and join him. When Elise had put the plantains and the ingredients in the pot, she came and sat near him. Immediately his arms went round her. She turned, smiled at him and rested her head on his shoulder. They were in that position for a while.

"Ralph, why don't you say something?" Elise asked.

"What should I say? Just being here with you is all I want." They sat quietly each wondering what the other was thinking.

The aroma of the ingredients boiling with the plantains assailed their nostrils and Elise got up to go and stir the contents of the pot. The aroma had aroused pangs of hunger in Ralph. He waited with such relish that he wondered whether he had ever waited for food so anxiously. Over the meal of porridge plantains they made small talk. Engaged in her words, Ralph also followed her gestures and facial expressions. No movement escaped him. He no longer looked at her from the patient-nurse point of view. From a closer range he savoured her, not allowing any intruding thoughts to disturb him.

He was lying on the double sitter with his leg stretched over the other end and his head resting on Elise's lap. They felt satisfied both with the food and with each other.

At two thirty, Russell returned to his house. Finding the door locked he went to look for the key where he usually hid it. On the table was a note for him. "Meet us at Elise's house." He read the note and sat down still looking at it. He did not know whether to be happy or sad. He was happy for his friend and sad because he was not that lucky.

Ralph and Elise were in the same position when Russell knocked and entered. His presence made Elise uncomfortable and she made to get up but Ralph pressed her back. Russell looked at them with a broad grin taking the place of greetings. Elise just had to get up.

"I see you two are very comfortable," Russell remarked.

"You too should be comfortable," Elise said as she pulled out a chair for him to sit down. "You must be hungry and tired.

We have eaten already. We were too hungry and could not wait for you." Russell dwelled on the recurrent we in Elise's words and wondered whether his friend had made his pronouncement.

But in this certainty of love a dark cloud lingered. The fact that she was an orphan and did not want to talk about her parentage mystified Russell and he wondered what his friend was going to do about this situation. He hoped that Ralph had not made the mistake of declaring his intentions without finding out Who Elise really was.

Ralph spent two more days in Bamenda during which he was assured that Elise loved him. He spent most part of the day with Elise, and only went back to Russell's house to sleep. He hoped Elise would suggest that he spend even one night in her house, but she didn't. He too was afraid to ask lest she jump to conclusions about his intentions. She was so natural in her response to his questions that at times he felt ashamed for asking them. She made sure he was happy but was careful not to overdo it or fuss over him. He tried to know more about her family to no avail. All she told him was that her mother died when she gave birth to her. At times she even enjoyed being the mystery woman. Even if she wanted to tell him about her family, what was she going to say? That she was not an orphan, that she had a father she had never seen? That was ridiculous. If Ralph loved her, then he should love her as she was.

The last night that Ralph spent in Bamenda he confided in his friend.

"Russell I have something in my mind which I must tell you before I go. You are the only person in a position to help me. I am very serious about Elise. But her avoidance of talking about her parentage worries me. I want you to do me a favour. If you can discreetly find out about her, I would be very grateful."

Russell smiled with relief. At least his friend was being reasonable and rational about this whole affair.

"I'll see what I can do."

"Please write and tell me as soon as you have any information. I have to report in at my new office next week As soon as I start working it will be difficult to come often to Bamenda. You know, I'm going to have my first experience working in an office. You are already a veteran at it. I can't imagine what it will be like."

"There is nothing particular about work in an office. You just have to get used to the routine. You come to the office every morning, go through the papers on your desk, meet new people make new friends, etc. That's about it."

I hope my documents in public service will move fast. I cannot wait to have the dough, man. To be really on your own must be something. I still have to ask my mom for cash. That is not easy. At times I feel bad about it but there is nothing I can do for now."

"Take it easy man. Being at the capital, at the source, you will soon have more than enough at your disposal. Then when I visit you I will be given red carpet treatment." Both of them started laughing.

"You are kidding man. Where do you think I'll get all that dough? For now I do not think it'll be much."

"Is there only one source?" Russell asked.

"How many sources are there? There is just my salary alone."

"You will find out. Just keep your eyes and ears open."

If marriage were a sort of game of chance, then Ralph had dipped his hand into the devil's mailbag, was holding the paper in his hand and planning the next move without knowing what was written on the piece of paper. He was so sure of winning that all other thoughts were dispelled as he mulled over his dreams.

Ralph arrived at his mother's house in a good mood. Claudette was in the kitchen helping Sam prepare supper. Sam opened the door for him and helped him carry his bag into his room. He was happy that Ralph could move on his own again. He looked cheerful in spite of the strain of the journey. In his room with Sam, he could hear movements in the kitchen.

"Who's in the kitchen? Has mama come back so early?"

"It is Claudette. Madam asked her to come and help cook supper," Sam replied and from the expression on his face it was evident that he was not happy with this arrangement. From the fleeting expression of surprise and annoyance that passed over Ralph's face, Sam could easily tell that his master was not happy with the situation either.

Back in the kitchen, Claudette knew it was Ralph but did not know how he was going to react to her presence. So she listened for his footsteps as he came out of his room. As soon as he appeared she rushed to him.

"You are looking great and your real self again," she remarked as she planted kisses on his cheeks. Ralph tried to put on an amiable smile, but inside he recoiled from her touch. "I was washing plantain stains from my hands. That's why I didn't come out immediately to welcome you. I see you are quite recovered."

"I am fine," Ralph replied in an indifferent voice as he turned to go back into the parlour. Claudette dropped the towel with which she was wiping her hands and followed him. He went and sat on the sofa and she came and sat beside him. He immediately regretted his choice of seat. He was finding her presence disturbing. Her presence in the house was no longer that of a chanced visitor. They were not that familiar to each other to guarantee the type of questions she was asking. His responses were monosyllabic and the information she hoped to get from her disguised interest in him was not forthcoming. In order to keep him company, her conversation was becoming desultory and this exasperated him. He began to wonder at her real intention or that of his mother in inviting her to help in the cooking that evening. Ralph like many other men had not got the experience of how women schemed and plotted to entrap them, bind them and bend them to their will. Madam Essin was doing just this and thought that she was succeeding.

"I think I should go and have a bath and rest before supper."

"You do not know how happy I am to see you looking so well."

"I appreciate that," Ralph said as he walked into the room. Claudette watched as he walked away and wondered why this change in him.

Madam Essin and Claudette had become close friends. Theirs was that type of friendship that builds up over an insignificant situation. Madam Essin had arrived at her residence one evening with two heavy bags. After the departure of the taxi man, she stood looking around wondering how to get the two bags up to her house. This young lady had come along and offered to help her. This was very unusual and Madam was grateful for the offer. After she had deposited the bags, Madam Essin had asked her to stay for a while. While they were sharing some drinks, Madam Essin got to know more about her. Claudette was a familiar face in the vicinity, but Madam Essin had never really taken note of her. In their conversation it was revealed that Claudette had known Ralph at the university. After the drinks, Claudette had carried the glasses into kitchen and washed them. This had given Madam Essin time to rest her wearied legs. She was surprised that a girl of her age could be so humble and helpful. Very few girls would do what she had done. To her this was a sign of responsibility. She really appreciated this and watched Claudette's every movement. In her heart, Madam saw the ideal daughter-in-law in her. Claudette was beautiful in her own way. Her greatest attribute was her shape, which Madam Essin admired. She had a mannequin's shape and no matter what she did, even child bearing would not make her lose it.

It was a beaming Madam Essin who embraced her son with all the affection a mother could display towards a grown up son. Claudette's presence too had enhanced the expectations in her heart. She had found them sitting together in the parlour, not together, but both were reading a magazine. The homely atmosphere gladdened her heart. Their presence had an effect on her, which she could not explain. During supper, Ralph was attentive to their every word, movement and facial expression. They in their turn were attentive to his every need and passed over dishes to him, filling his glass and encouraging him to eat more. He observed these gestures with indignant amusement. The women chatted as they ate and Ralph responded in short sentences. He was not interested in what they were saying but did not want to appear uninterested. Not much had been said about his journey to Bamenda and Madam Essin was contented that her son had overcome his infatuation over the nurse he had met at the hospital. Ralph's mind was in Bamenda but they attributed his silence to tiredness and soon left him alone.

Ralph's life was taking a new turn. He went out more often visiting friends and places he had not seen for five years. He felt something stirring in him as his consciousness became liberated from the cloister of his convalescence. He did everything to avoid Claudette but could not succeed. He avoided her because he did not want to give his mother any reason for her hopes to look positive. He was not interested in Claudette and did not want to give her any hope either. His mother had been making all the suggestions and decisions. He had allowed her to do this while he hid behind the cloak of his convalescence. But now that he was on his feet he was not going to allow his mother to boss him anymore. He dreaded ever having to meet Claudette on the street. He did not want to be rude to her by rejecting her company; neither did he want to invite her attention. Claudette had gotten the misconception, maybe from Madam Essin, that Ralph would not want to hurt her so Claudette had tried to make suggestions to accompany Ralph on some of his visits. But Ralph had insisted on going to these places alone to be able to enjoy the company of his friends without her interfering presence. He just loved to move around the streets watching the people moving up and down. He went to the main shops like Score and many of the shops along Monte Ane Rouge. One morning he was coming down from Marché Central towards the French Cultural Centre when he met Claudette on the street. He did not know that her office was around there. He had seen her approaching but there was no way for him to escape for she had already seen him and was smiling at him as she moved towards him.

"Hi, it's so nice to see you again," Claudette said as they shook hands and then Claudette kissed him on the cheeks. "I am sure you have not started work yet. What are you doing in town? Well, I should not be asking you this question. You want to get a feel of the town again." It was midday and she was going to her favourite restaurant to eat. So she invited him to join her. He had no tangible reason to give her for not wanting to accompany her so he went along.

This was two weeks after his return from Bamenda. Her visits had become less frequent and his earlier suspicions were allayed but meeting her again, he still wanted to get to the bottom of this intimate friendship she had with his mother.

"What will you have?" she asked when they were seated.

"Anything you order," Ralph replied.

"We will have some drinks first. You are surely not taking drugs so I will order for us." To the waiter she said, "Two bottles of Tuburg please."

"Oh no, no please. No beer for me. If you do not mind, I will have a bottle of pamplemousse."

"Men who do not drink beer are rare nowadays. Why don't you drink beer?" she asked.

"Well, I just don't take to it."

"For health reasons?"

"I just can't get myself used to it."

"You haven't tried hard enough."

"That is not something to try hard for. There is no harm in avoiding alcohol."

"I hope you remain steadfast in your resolution, it will be very good." To a male observer, they made an odd couple with the woman drinking the beer and the man drinking the soft drink. When their drinks arrived she asked for the menu of the day. It was brought and they made their choices. Claudette chose yam and ndole while Ralph chose corn fufu with huckleberry. He had developed a liking for this dish during his brief stay in Bamenda.

Over their drinks they talked about a number of issues. Then after a brief pause Claudette said, "You know I like you. I like your company. I hope this has not come as a surprise to you. I also like your mother very much. She is like a mother to me and I would do anything to make her happy."

"So this was it," Ralph thought. He did not answer but kept looking at her. Their eyes met but she could not hold his gaze. She covered up with a smile and stumbled on.

"Am I not beautiful? Why do you treat me as if I am not a woman?" This had come out as if she could not control herself any longer, and when it was out, she did not look pleased at all.

"I am sorry Claudette if I have treated you badly. It was not intentional. You are a nice woman." He did not continue and she could see from his face that he was angry.

"Let us talk about something else. I am sorry I brought this up." Their food was brought and placed before them, but Ralph had lost his appetite. He no longer enjoyed the food, as he would have because of the uneasy silence that hung over them. When they asked for the bill, it was brought and placed besides Ralph. He made no move to take it. But how could he? He had no such amount on him. Claudette without looking at him took the bill and placed the money in the tray. This was not strange but to Ralph it made him look inadequate. His five years in France had not wiped away the fact that he was an African and in Africa, it was always the man who provided. Their meeting had provided him with what he wanted to verify. She had asked him why he could not treat her like a woman. That meant going further than he was. He could clearly see his mother's hand in all that had been happening.

That evening, Ralph went early to bed. Tired from the walking he had done during the day he needed an early rest. As soon as he got into bed, he put off the lights. He had not fallen asleep when there was a knock on his door. He knew it was his mother and wondered what she wanted. She scarcely came to his room and he appreciated this. His mother had not broached the topic of marriage since she last talked about it in Bamenda. He had a premonition that she was coming now to talk about it. He prepared himself not to be uncompromising. If it were something else, then it had to be serious enough for her to come to her room to talk about it. He listened as she talked about the merits of getting married and how his marriage would be the fulfilment of her life's dream. Although she did not mention Claudette's name, he did not want her to go without his confirming his thoughts now that she had brought it up.

"Mother, do you think a girl like Claudette would make a good wife for me?"

"Well, I like her and she is a good girl and quiet helpful. But it all depends on you." She looked thoughtful for some time and continued, "But what do you think of her? It's your decision to make."

"I will think about it mother." He yawned as he said this indicating that the conversation was over.

In spite of his tiredness, Ralph could not sleep. He turned and tossed, his mind preoccupied with the possible consequences of what he was about to do. Russell had not written to him yet and he was afraid of giving himself away to his mother. She would be forewarned and forearmed. This was dangerous. He wanted to take her by surprise. Mentally and physically exhausted he fell asleep and slept until 9 am. His mother had left for the shop wondering why he was not yet up but she dared not go and wake him up. The sleep had not been refreshing. He got up feeling generally tired and weak. He took a cold bath and dressed for breakfast. At the table, he poured a cup of coffee and took a sip. Then he sat and stared through the window. He forgot about the cup of coffee and it got cold.

"Can I pour you another cup of coffee?" Sam asked, his voice interrupting his thoughts.

"Thanks Sam, I have had enough," Ralph answered, coming back to the realities around him. He got up suddenly and went into his room. He got out a sheet of paper and took out a pen from his briefcase and returned to the dining room. When he started writing, the pen crawled over the pages without stopping. When he got to the end he heaved a deep sigh of relief. He read it over quickly, folded the paper and put it in an envelope. The haste with which he carried out this action indicated that he did not want to go back on the decision he had taken. In the same manner he got up, moved over to where he had kept his newly bought Samara bag, put the letter inside and walked out. The determined look on his face left Sam wondering what was wrong with his master.

6

There had been changes in the work schedule and nurses were transferred from one ward to another. Elise had been moved from the New Private Ward to the Postnatal Ward. The patients were all women and their ailments varied. There was much more work to be done. Doing rounds with the doctor in the morning, washing babies and carrying out discharge procedures kept her on her legs during her daytime shift of work. During night duty, the cries of babies and the constant call to attend to mothers in pain or to remove and change drip sets were telling on her. In her former ward, she had more time to rest, for the patients were mostly adults who behaved well except in crisis situations.

When the body is active, the mind is preoccupied. During the first week after Ralph's departure, Elise did not have much time to think about him. When he had left with the plaster on his leg, she had received a letter from him within the first week. But after the second departure, the week was almost running out and there was no letter. The week came and went, still no letter. The weekend was uneventful. The second week began. There was still no letter. She was beginning to doubt the reality of all that had happened when Ralph was with her. She kept herself as busy as she could to avoid having thinking of the possibilities of what might have happened when Ralph went back to Yaounde.

On Thursday morning she arrived at the hospital and changed into her nurse's uniform. She moved round with the nurses who had been on night duty to carry out the handing over procedures. "Today is another day," she said to herself as she washed the babies and handed them over to her partner for cleaning and treatment of the stump of the umbilical cords. Handling the babies, she imagined how she herself must have looked as a baby. She marvelled at the fact that it takes two to make one. As she worked her mind roved. What was it in people that made them choose each other out of the thousands of men and women around them? Wait a minute, what was it that had attracted her to Ralph? Why did she feel towards him the way she did? The squeal of a baby distracted her and ended this trend of thought. The washing was over and there was some quiet in the ward as the babies were fed and some sleeping. The relatives, husbands and in-laws were already queuing up for discharge formalities for the women who were strong enough to go home. There were bills to be paid and certificates to be signed. Elise was busy filling out birth forms when a letter was dropped before her on the table. The nurse distributing letters was a humorous lady. The remark she made as she walked away left Elise giggling. The handwriting on the envelope was familiar so she put the letter into her handbag. She did not have many people who wrote to her. Her aunt wrote occasionally. Her friends in secondary school wrote now and then. But since she had known Ralph, she had been receiving such long letters and often too. The letter she had just received was from Ralph and she did not want to read it while at work. She liked to read letters from Ralph in an environment where she could peruse and reflect on the contents without interruption. Her colleagues had noticed this attitude and remarked that she was very unresponsive. They expected her to express some excitement. Elise could control her emotions in the presence of other people, but alone they erupted. She hugged herself uncontrollably, placed the letter on her chest and gazed into space, conjuring pleasant images and smiling to herself. This particular letter from Ralph was more than she could bear.

All the tender words and particularly what he was asking of her brought tears of happiness into her eyes. Her dreams had come true. At last, here was the man for her. She was so happy that she did not want anything to cloud her joy. She had to tell her aunt. Who else should share in her joy apart from her aunt? She thought of the fastest means to communicate with her. A letter would take too long. Her aunt had to know immediately. Elise was also dying to know what her aunt would say about her marriage to Ralph. She had depended on her aunt for advice on whatever steps she wanted to take. But now she had taken a decision on her own. Telephoning was the easiest and fastest means. She searched for the telephone number of a family she knew in Buea. She asked them to inform her aunt that she would like to talk with her at four o'clock the next day. She had to come to that house to receive the call. That night, Elise could not sleep. Her happiness was suffocating and she felt restless. She did not know what to do with herself. She read and reread Ralph's letter. The next day she spoke with her aunt. Elise wanted her to come so that they could discuss something. Aunt Pauline arrived in Bamenda at 5 am. She could not rest after speaking with Elise. Elise had sounded more excited than sick. There was a tight knot at the bottom of her stomach and she kept jumping from one possibility to another. Elise had not as much as hinted at why she wanted to see her. She had just said that it was urgent and important. Aunt Pauline after thinking about it concluded that it must be in connection with her father.

Elise was on afternoon shift so she was still in her bed when Aunt Pauline arrived. At her knock Elise's heartbeat accelerated. She knew it was her aunt because nobody knocked at her door so early in the morning. As Elise greeted and fussed over her, Aunt Pauline looked at her closely. She had never seen Elise so excited. Her eyes sparkled and she stumbled over her words in her excitement. She wanted her aunt to be as comfortable as possible.

"You must be hungry. You must be cold. Let me warm some water for you to take a bath."
"Don't worry. Buea is as cold as Bamenda. Let me have a rest first." As Elise moved about arranging her bed and tidying up her room, she kept up a flow of questions about everybody she knew in Buea. Aunty Pauline looked round the parlour. She was impressed at Elise's level of maturity. Elise had been interested in making her parlour comfortable in a simple way. There was a double sitter and two singles all made of cane. She had made them more comfortable by putting additional pillows at the corners. A plastic carpet to match gave the parlour a cosy look. Her responsibility could not be seen only in what her parlour looked like. She had sent her aunt money a number of times. She had also sent her raw food like beans, cabbages and carrots

88

when any of her friends were going to Buea. As Aunt Pauline thought of all these she marvelled at the independence of human beings. Not many years back, Elise was dependent on her for everything. Now she was on her own and Aunt Pauline was satisfied that she had done her best.

It was 8 O'clock and they had potato chips and eggs for breakfast. They were talking about trivialities when her aunt could not contain herself anymore.

"Elise, you have grown into a woman, a responsible woman."

"Thank you aunty." Elise replied and got up to embrace her.

"But you have not told me why you called for me. It must be something quite important." She smiled at her, convinced that what Elise had to say must be in connection with her father.

"Yes aunty, it is quite important. I do not know where to begin." Aunt Pauline held her breath, for Elise's face had become downcast and serious. "I had this patient in the hospital…" Elise narrated all that had transpired between her and Ralph. "Three days ago, I received a letter from him asking me to marry him." Silence…silence. Elise bowed her head when she made the last statement. She was suddenly frightened after saying it. She did not want to see the expression on her aunt's face. Why was her aunt not responding to what she had said? She wondered. The sound of the chair being pulled back made her take up her head. Her aunt came to sit by her.

"Elise, I am so happy for you. But who is this young man? Marriage is not just between two people. It is between two families. So you realize that we must know his family. What is his name?" When Aunt Pauline heard the details that Elise could furnish, she stayed quiet for some time, her mind diving back into the archives of the past.

"You say that his mother's name is Perpetua Essin? Has he got any brothers or sisters?"

"No aunty, he is an only child." Aunt Pauline's mind was raking the archives desperately. Since the incident of Elise's mother's death, the family had picked up scraps of information here and there, and as she recalled them, Perpetua Essin and

Ralph's mother were one and the same person. This was the son of the Perpetua Essin who was believed to have killed Elise's mother! Aunt Pauline's blood ran cold. This was not possible. She wondered why fate should treat her so. She looked at Elise and did not know what to say. As the silence continued Elise looked more and more frightened. She felt sorry for Elise for not knowing the truth, while she held the truth in her heart. She thought she had locked that knowledge in her heart and thrown away the key. She now had no choice but to unlock it and let Elise know the truth. It was a painful decision. How was Elise going to receive it? She might hate her for hiding the truth from her, hiding the fact that she had a father, cousins and aunts.

"Elise, what I am going to tell you will hurt you. I do not like doing it but I have no choice. This Perpetua Essin, Ralph's mother…"

That weekend Andre went to Yaounde to tell his parents that he had finally made up his mind to get married. This came as a shock to them as they knew that his wife had one more year in the university before they would get married.

"So you had not made up your mind?" his mother asked. "What about Emiliene?"

"Did I say I was going to marry her? Look, mother, am I not big enough to choose my own wife?"

"When we talked to you about Emiliene, did you not understand that we wanted you to marry her?"

"Did I say yes? And since then, have I done anything to show that I am interested?"

"What about all the money we've spent on her and the gifts to her parents?" The mother asked with venom in her voice.

"It was your money and your gifts not mine."

"How can you leave a girl who will soon leave university?" The mother half pleaded. The weekend had been spoiled for Andre and in his exasperation he did not want to face his father. He took a bus back to Douala.

Two months later Anne became pregnant and when Andre's parents heard that he had made a woman pregnant and wanted to marry her, they flew into a rage. They had not gotten over this when they heard that Andre spent all his time in Tiko. They gathered their forces and waited to see what steps he was going to take next. He could not go alone to marry a woman. He needed some elders in the family to do the initial approach for him.

Andre was the third child in a family of six. His father had left his native village of Bakan in the Western Province of the country to come to Yaounde. It was in the early sixties when Cameroon had just got independence and there were many job opportunities in Yaounde. As a young man, he had his future before him. With his C.E.P, he got a job as a messenger in the Ministry of National Education. Working with people who dealt with students he was motivated to study for his BEPC. With this qualification he was promoted to Chef du Bureau. With a stable job, he went home and got a wife. As he became a family man other members of the family came to live with him. His success in Yaounde was an eye opener to many young men in the village and they too left the village for Yaounde. Over the years many more family members came to join them and a good number were now settled in Yaounde. In their struggle for survival in a strange city they stuck together and always came together for family meetings. They shared in each other's problems and successes. It was the whole extended family that determined any important course of action to be taken by any individual. Andre was trying to break this tradition.

In her eighth month of pregnancy Anne took her maternity leave and Andre advised her to come and stay with him in Douala where he would be around to rush her to the hospital when the time came. Anne's parents knew that their daughter was pregnant but as far as they were concerned their daughter was not yet married. Andre had met them and explained that he wanted to marry Anne but they had insisted that she should give birth first before anything could be done. Andre could not persuade them to the contrary and since Anne was pregnant, he thought there was no need to hurry. Anne herself was assured that everything was going to be fine and told her parents not to be afraid that Andre wouldn't take care of her. They believed she was mature enough to know what she wanted. Andre also wanted to be around when his first child was born. When his family got to know about this from the spy network they had set up, Aunt Perpetua opted to be the spokesperson for the family and decided to pay Andre a visit.

"So you are the queen fit for Andre?" Perpetua asked after she had inspected Anne from her feet to her head. When Perpetua had come in, she had not asked for Andre or who Anne was.

"And who are you?" Anne asked.

"You want to know who I am? You will know when you are no longer in this house." It was at this moment that Anne realized that this must be one of Andre's relatives and took her time.

"What is this I am seeing?" Perpetua continued. "A bellyful of beans water or pregnancy? I will see where this will end." When Perpetua realized that her words had no effect on Anne she made her attacks more poignant.

"Do you know that you are not wanted in this house? A mere grade two teacher."

At this Anne was hurt. "If I am not wanted in this house, then what do you think I am doing here? I know why I am here. Andre also knows. So what is your problem?" Perpetua had been disconcerted by this cool response. She had been ready for a quarrel and eventually a fight. She knew that a pregnant woman no matter her strength was not a match for her.

"I am sorry for you. If I were the one I would not stay in this house. Our family does not want you as a wife. Andre is not an island. He cannot marry a wife alone. He alone cannot stand against his whole family. You will not succeed in this. Let me assure you."

In spite of her plan to devastate Anne, Perpetua was struck by her beauty, the moment Anne appeared. Some women are so beautiful that some other women honestly admire them. Under normal circumstances, Perpetua could have done the same, but she glared at Anne and banged the door after her when she went out.

Anne had been living with Andre for three weeks and was at the beginning of her eighth month of pregnancy when this happened. Before narrating the incident to Andre, Anne had taken the decision to go back to Victoria to be with her parents when she gave birth.

"I think it will be better for me to go back to Victoria and give birth there. I do not feel safe here anymore," Anne concluded after narrating the events of that morning.

"Please Anne, so long as I am here nothing will happen to you. Please have confidence in me. I love you," Andre replied.

"I know you love me and I love you too. I would like you to be present when our baby is born. But you cannot stand against your family."

"That is not true Anne. You know that together we can withstand all odds. The way we shall live will convince them that we were meant for each other."

"I know that Andre. But I still want to go back to Victoria. Before and after I give birth, there will be much to be done and you alone cannot handle it. Let me go to my parents. I will come back as soon as I am strong enough."

Andre saw reason in what she had said and two days after, Anne was back in Victoria.

Her parents were happy to see her. When they heard what had happened they became worried but Anne assured them that things were going to be fine. Andre had all along acted in a way that all their fears that their daughter was going to have a child with an irresponsible man were dispelled. He had even told them that he was ready to go and sign the marriage certificate while Anne was still pregnant. But her parents had thought otherwise. They wanted to get to know their in-laws better first.

Anne was sitting in front of their house one evening when an old woman who was their neighbour two buildings away passed by and saw her.

"Anne my daughter, how are you feeling?"

"Mbamba, I am fine." The old woman sat down beside Anne.

"I can see that you are fine. Thank God. This is your first pregnancy, I am sure."

"Yes, Mbamba. How do you know?"

"I just asked. I did not know. You look more beautiful with this pregnancy."

"Thank you Mbamba."

"Have you been washed?"

"Mbamba, how is one washed?"

"Iya...eh!" the old woman exclaimed." So Martina has not done anything? Let me see her. I will talk to her seriously. Come tomorrow and see me. A woman in her first pregnancy has to be washed."

When Anne's mother heard about it, she said it was a good idea, but thought that Anne would not be interested.

The next evening, Anne went to see the old woman. They had to wait for the woman's daughter-in-law to finish cooking before they could use the firewood kitchen. While Anne waited, the daughter-in law told her of the merits of such treatment before delivery. It was dusk when they started the procedure. The old woman had got all the herbs ready. There was the bark of the mangrove tree. This she placed at the bottom of the pot. As she arranged the leaves and roots of the various medicinal plants, she told Anne about each of them. It was a big lesson for Anne as she learnt the names of many plants in the Bakweri mother tongue. Finally the old woman set the pot on the fire and poured water in it until all the contents were covered. She did not cover the pot with a lid. She placed a thick towel over it. As the water became hot and started boiling, the towel became damp. She asked Anne to undress. Anne pulled off her kaba and was left only with her pant. She asked Anne to sit nearer the fire and expose her stomach to the heat. She took the warm towel and covered Anne's stomach with it. She palpated her stomach muttering to herself. She did this three times. When the herbs were boiled she lifted the pot and put it on the floor to cool. She poured out the greenish liquid and gave her some to drink. It was bitter but had a sweet aftertaste. This she explained was to relax the pubic bones and clear the passage way for the child. The next evening when Anne came again, there was another concoction. This was used as enema to keep the bowels clear and allow the child free movement. Anne came to her for five days. When the treatment was complete, she showed Anne some leaves to use every two days as enema until she gave birth. Anne had become used to being with the old woman in the evenings. When there was nothing more to be done, she spoke about the days when she was a young woman. There are some old people who love to relive their past experiences through conversation. Anne was a patient listener and asked questions that only led to other series of stories. The old woman loved this.

Andre visited Anne twice a week bringing along all she needed. Money was not a problem. Andre was so excited about becoming a father that only his job kept him away from Victoria. On one of his visits Aunt Perpetua secretly followed him to Victoria. After his departure Perpetua came to the house and gave Anne and her mother a good telling off. She reminded them that they were not going to succeed in their plans and the marriage was not going to take place because their family would never allow it. She reminded Anne that she was going to give birth to a bastard. During Andre's next visit Anne told him what had happened keeping away the abuses and the foul language she had used. Andre was so angry that he threatened to have nothing to do with his family if they interfered in his life. Anne calmed him down saying that she knew of many couples whose parents were against their marriage but the man and the woman showed them that they were determined to live as husband and wife. Eventually the families had left them alone and even visited them later to apologize.

Two weeks after this incident, Andre was sent to Yaounde to take part in a seminar organized by their company. The seminar was to last a week. Before leaving, he promised to steal time off during the seminar to come and see her. Anne still had ten days to her expected delivery date, so there was no need to worry.

The same day Andre left for Yaounde, Anne went to visit the old woman. "Mbamba, you have done so much for me. Look at how you have taken care of me without asking for anything."

"Never mind my child, I am getting old and love to see babies born. Whenever I look at a newborn baby, I say to myself, that one will continue where I left off." Anne laughed but the laughter was caught in her throat. She had felt a sharp pain in

95

her lower abdomen and had grimaced in pain. She did not know what was happening but the old woman had seen the pain in her face. The old woman set about preparing an enema. She put some water on the fire and went out to get the leaves that went into the concoction. Anne was not alarmed because she had done this several times during the past weeks. But when the old woman declared that this was the last enema she was giving Anne, she was alarmed and asked.

"Am I in labour? Are these labour pains?"

"Yes my daughter."

"No, it cannot be. The nurses say I have to give birth at the end of next week. I still have many more days to go."

"The nurses are right. But they are not God. Just prepare and go to the hospital. At times it starts like this and stops for some days. It is better to go to the hospital."

Before Anne left the old woman said, "Have courage my daughter, you are going to give birth to a baby girl and you should call her Elisa. She is going to be my mboombo. That is all I ask you to give me."

"Thank you, mbamba. I promise I will name her after you."

Two hours later Anne was in the hospital in active labour. It was not an easy one. Anne's mother as well as the old woman had come to the hospital to give her moral support. They were not allowed to see her as soon as she was taken into the labour ward. The labour was painful and not progressing as expected. She was injected with some Syntocinon to help the contractions on. At two a.m. Anne gave birth to a baby girl. The labour had tired her out as well as the baby. The baby was taken to the nursery for observation while Anne was left in the labour ward for observation, because she was bleeding abnormally. The doctor was called immediately and another injection, this time Methegin, was administered. A pint of blood was transfused and the bleeding showed signs of abating. Her mother heaved a sigh of relieve when Anne was wheeled out of the labour ward to the postnatal ward. She had drips on both arms, glucose on one and blood on the other.

That afternoon, Anne managed to eat and talk. That evening the bleeding started again and Anne died quietly in her sleep. The family was uncertain whether to call for Andre or not. More to that, they did not know how to contact him. They knew of the office where he worked in Douala but did not know how to contact him in Yaounde. If they had called his office not much could be achieved because they did not know he had a wife. Some members of the family did not want to have anything to do with him because they believed his family was responsible for her death. This belief firmly took root and soon there was a general consensus that Andre would never see the baby. Anne was buried two days later at the Victoria cemetery and the whole neighbourhood mourned her.

Elise listened with a beating heart, her pulse racing. She suffered the greatest disillusionment in her life. As she listened to the events that led to her birth and her mother's death, her faith in the whole of human nature was rudely and callously shattered, leaving her alone and defenceless in a deceitful and dishonest world.

"...so you cannot marry him," her aunt concluded.

Elise heard this last statement from afar. She sat like a statue, in a void, empty of emotions, staring at her aunt. She was incapable of speech or any reaction. She could not cry. She was stiff from immobility. Without a word, Elise got up and walked into her room. Her aunt was left in the parlour alone. Her mind too was in turmoil. She could not believe the turn events had taken. Her thoughts kept wandering and she could not dwell on any. They kept fleeting as if they did not want to be entrapped and exploited further. Not succeeding in getting any idea on how to alleviate both her situation and Elise's predicament, she thought just being near her would show her that the family had not acted with evil intentions but to protect her. She got up and went into the room. Elise was lying across the bed staring at the ceiling. Her motionless figure and unblinking eyes frightened her. Aunt Pauline sat beside her and held her hand. Elise screamed, jumped up and ran to the door. Aunt Pauline gripped her and held her tight against her chest. Elise's tears gushed out and her sobs raked her body. The anaesthetic state of her emotions had caused a lethargic reaction, giving way to a frenzy of uncontrolled activity triggered by her aunt's touch. They struggled in silence and her aunt succeeded in putting her back on the bed. Her sobs turned into a sorrowful whimpering. This went on for such a long time that the aunt wondered whether things were really normal with the child. Elise muttered some words and fell asleep. Aunt Pauline sat by her wondering what to do next. She wondered whether talking to her about her father would give her some hope and reason for living. Did the man in question know what was in store for him? She wondered. What was his mother's reaction to all this? Did she know who Elise is? These questions revolved round in her head and tired her out mentally and physically. She too soon fell into a restless sleep. She did not know for how long she had slept when a whimpering sound woke her up. Elise was tossing on her side of the bed. Aunt Pauline did not know how to start talking to Elise. She was afraid of what Elise would say to her. She wanted to comfort her and tell her that it was not the end of the world and that she still had a father who at last wanted her. But she did not dare broach the topic of her father. She got up and sat looking round the room. Elise got up and went to her valise. She opened it and lifted her dresses until she got to the bottom. She pulled out an envelope and went into the parlour. As she sat rereading the letter from her father, her heart constricted with pain and she considered herself the most unfortunate child on earth. There were no answers to her whys so she made up her mind.

From instinct, she looked at her watch. It showed twenty minutes to two and she was supposed to be on the afternoon shift of work, which began at two o'clock. She got up took a bucket of water that stood at the back of the door and went into the bathroom. As she bathed she made her plans. Knowledge of the past had pivoted her into a different situation. It was not a pleasant one but she decided she was going to continue living for as long as she was alive. She was going to forge ahead. When the lord closes the door, somewhere he opens a window. She remembered that Maria had said that in The Sound of Music and that expression had always given her hope. There was a window opened for her somewhere and she was going to pass through it.

As she went through the motions of preparing for work her aunt observed. Her normally smooth black face was creased. Her lips were dry and cracked and occasionally trembled. Her every action denoted a preoccupied mind. As Aunt Pauline watched, her heart went out to her. Elise had left her watch on the cane cupboard in the room, and when she wanted to go out she could not remember where it was. She went in and out of the room lifting and looking under things. She did not utter a word all this while. Her aunt had seen the watch and knew that that was what she was looking for.

"Are you looking for your watch? It is under the comb on the cane cupboard." Elise turned and looked at her as if she did not know that she was in the room with her. She picked up her watch and walked out.

She arrived at the hospital ten minutes late and the nurses from whom she had to take over duties were already impatient. Elise dropped her bag and put on her nurse's gown. She did not respond to the questions posed to her. It seemed as if she had lost the ability to speak. The nurses found this strange and the strained pallor of Elise's face told them there was something wrong. But since she did not want to speak, they left her alone. She went through the handing over procedures like a robot. The first patient who needed her attention was a baby whose drip had finished and had to be replaced. She carried the tray to the bedside and managed to replace the drip set. On her way back to the nurse's station, there was a sudden pain at the back of her neck. Suddenly she could not see. Her vision was blurred. She felt for the wall to support herself. She let go of the tray and it went crashing to the floor. Her knees buckled under her and she went down. A passing visitor saw her falling and screamed. The other nurses left what they were doing and rushed to her. Patients, nurses and visitors all crowded around her. The crowd was still gathering when the nurses carried her into their station and laid her on the bed there. They were frantic, trying to revive her. Her pulse was irregular. They tried to resuscitate her. For twenty minutes she lay motionless. Gradually she came round, hearing noises as if from afar but coming nearer. She heard her name being called and she answered in a weak voice. A doctor was called and he examined her carefully. Her vital signs were positive but she was very weak. He ordered for a glucose drip to be transfused. When all was quiet, Elise's partner went and stood outside with two other nurses. They wondered what had happened. Since Elise had been secretive about her relationship with Ralph, they did not have anything on this premise. Elise had to spend the night at the hospital not on duty but as a patient, so she needed some clothing and bed sheets. At nine p.m. when the nurses were going home one of them offered to go to Elise's house and bring the things she needed. There was no key in Elise's bag and she could not tell them that there was somebody at home. The nurse took the chance to still go to her house. When she got there she noticed that the lights were on so thought there must be someone in the room. She knocked and entered.

"I have come to take some clothes and beddings for Elise."

"Is she spending the night there? She was to come back. That is what she told me." The nurse explained what had happened and the aunt exclaimed.

"Iya.e.e.e! Let us go and see her. Iya e.e.e!"

On the way to the hospital Aunt Pauline talked to herself the whole time but the nurse could not understand what she was saying because she was speaking in her mother tongue, the Bakweri language. Elise was lying on her bed looking pale and haggard. Aunt Pauline burst into tears at the sight and was taken outside.

Elise had always talked about her aunt but the few nurses who knew her were not on duty that evening. Between sobs she told them who she was and they tried to console her. She wept from the depths of her being. Hers was that soul raking tears that issue from an adult in complete despair. She wept not only because of Elise but also because of so many other things. She thought of Elise's mother and wept. She thought of all she had gone through with the child and wept. She wept for herself. She knew she was going to lose Elise no matter what she did. In the moment of sorrow every other emotion is subdued, reasoning is put at bay and the mind goes on rampage. There was nothing seriously wrong with Elise, but human reaction to a state of helplessness evokes the end of the world. Aunt Pauline passed the night at the hospital sitting on a chair. She remembered how she had sat up night after night tending the screaming infant who had pulled and pulled at her nipples until lactation hormones were reactivated. She thought of the past. She thought of the present and the future. Those who have suffered much and endured a lot usually resign themselves to situations by withdrawing into themselves. The night was long and painful.

It was also a long and painful night for Andre many years ago when he learnt of the death of his beloved wife. He had endured a lot from his family's attitude towards his choice of a wife and had to endure much more when he lost her. His manner of resignation was to try and get himself away and to forget the pain. Andre came back from Yaounde the night Anne was buried. He had no idea of what had happened. He did not feel like doing anything. He felt melancholic as well as tired. He thought his melancholia was as a result of his not being able to get to Victoria that night to see his wife. He spent a restless night and the next day he was on his way to see her. When he stopped at the taxi park in Victoria, he felt a heaviness come over him. He walked slowly away from Half mile towards the side road that let to Anne's parent's home. Before he got there he saw Lawrence standing at the door of a provision store. He moved towards him. When the child saw him, he shouted.

"Uncle Andre!" he rushed to him and held him round his waist and burst into tears. "Aunty is dead," he wailed. Andre's bag fell to the ground and he staggered. The people around held him and made him sit on a bench.

"Please uncle do not go to the house. They say that it is that woman who killed her. That is why they do not want to see you. Please do not go. Please! Please!"

Andre kept his head between his palms and tried to control himself. He remembered his aunt's visit to his house in Douala. He remembered all the ill feeling that had existed between him and his family when news went round that he had confronted her. They had been particularly angered by the fact that he had told her that she was jealous because her husband had abandoned her. He could not go to see Anne's parents. He

101

knew they would not want to see him. After twenty minutes, Andre got control of himself but he was still in a daze.

"Where is she?" he asked. Lawrence did not understand what he meant and gave him the answer he knew.

"She has been buried."

Andre could not help himself anymore.

"So they could not even wait for me to see her for the last time?" He wailed openly.

"Where is the cemetery?

"I will take you there. But let me go home and give this bread before I come with you."

"Do not tell them I am here," Andre pleaded.

At the cemetery Andre burst into uncontrolled tears and fell on the freshly dug earth.

"Anne! Anne! Why have you done this to me? Why! Why! My life was complete with you. Now there is nothing for me. My world is empty without you," he wailed.

Lawrence had never seen a man weeping so openly. He pitied Andre and tried to console him in his childlike manner. When Andre had regained control of himself he asked about the child.

"It is a girl. Mama has taken her to Buea. They say that none of you will ever see the child. Uncle, please go away. People at the store might have gone to tell them you are here. Uncle, please go away. They can come and kill you."

"Yes Lawrence, I will go away but I will come back. I must come back. I cannot believe she is gone forever. Oh Anne! Anne!" They walked away in silence back to the road.

"Lawrence, you are my only friend left. I will come back to see you. Tell mama that I came and that I have seen Anne."

Lawrence could not understand what he meant by this and looked at Andre's receding back wondering whether he was normal.

Back in Douala, Andre spent a miserable day looking at Anne's picture and talking to her. He told all his dreams to the inanimate picture and something made him believe she heard and understood him. He felt so empty. The whole day he neither ate nor drank. The next day he managed to get out of bed. His clothes were rumpled and his eyes bloodshot. There was a three-day growth of hair on his chin but this did not bother him as he grieved for his lost love. He moved on the streets like a zombie. At a funereal shop, he bought a wreath of pure white roses. While the lady of the shop got the wreath ready she asked what words he would like on it. As if in a vision, he remembered the words he had spoken to Anne the first night he spent with her. "Don't leave me my darling."

Since the lady could not understand English he helped her choose the letters and arrange them on he wreath.

At five o'clock that evening a lonely figure was seen entering the Victoria cemetery. He held a large parcel in his arms and his steps seemed to be too heavy for him. He approached the grave where Anne was buried, unwrapped the wreath and placed it reverentially. He stood back and read the words to her. "Don't leave me my darling." But Anne was gone leaving him behind. She was gone but she was still alive in his memory. At that moment Andre convinced himself that she had not left him. With a heavy heart, with sobs threatening to overcome him, he retraced his steps out of the cemetery. In the gathering dusk there was a white blob on one of the freshly dug graves.

Andre stayed away from work for a week. Friends tried to console him when they heard what had happened. They advised him to no avail. The reaction from his family left him more desolate.

Three weeks after Anne's death, Andre was not still himself but he went to work and carried on like a robot. One afternoon he came back from work exhausted. He stretched out on the sofa to rest and fell asleep. He was not deeply asleep. He was dreaming. Anne and he were laughing at a joke he could not remember. Anne was radiant with life and happiness. He woke up with the cold realization that she was not with him. The rest of the afternoon was spoilt for him. He did not feel he could go back to work. He was in that state of melancholia when his colleague came in with a parcel for him.

Andre had applied for admission into a university in the United States of America. He had received no response when he expected it and had forgotten about it. One day, he received a letter, opened it, and found out he had been admitted. The letter had taken so long in transit that he had just a week to put the necessary documents together. Fortunately, the money he had been saving was still intact. This was a timely intervention from God as it got him out of his stupor into a frenzy of activity. When all was set and he had bought his ticket, he went to Yaounde to inform his parents. It was two days to his departure and he did not want any fuss. He was not in the mood to discuss anything with them and all effort by the family to make him understand that they had nothing to do with the death of the girl he wanted to marry was in vain. Nothing could make him believe the contrary. With his impending journey, his parents did not know whether to be happy or sad. He had become a complete stranger to them and with the recent tragedy, they did not know where to begin with him. He did not give them a chance to say anything. They consoled themselves with the fact that he would eventually get over it and accept Emiliene. They underestimated their son.

His flight was booked for the eighth of October. The evening before his departure, he visited Anne's grave and spoke with her.

"Anne, my love, you have left me alone in this world. I love you more than I will ever love any woman. Though you have gone, my love remains steadfast. I will never love any woman the way I love you." Andre drank himself to oblivion that night.

7

True to his word, Russell had done his job. There was this retired midwife who lived in his neighbourhood. He was one of the first men to venture into this field believed to be good only for women. He was taken to do the midwifery course at the Bamenda Midwifery School. After his course he was posted to go and work in Victoria. His experience in midwifery had gained him unequalled respect and the name Pa baby. He was called Pa baby because he was considered the father of all the babies he had delivered. Many babies had been named after him and one could see pride beaming on his face if a woman stopped to greet him and introduce a young man or woman as the baby he had delivered. To Pa Nchu [that was real name] everybody was "my daughter" or "my son." He had this fatherly aura around him to the extent that those who were almost his age did not resent him calling them so. Everybody felt at ease in his presence. He knew the secrets of many families who had come to him for help, advice or just to get a load out of their chest.

As a civil servant he had built a good house for himself first. As a native of Mankon he could get land easily especially in those days when the town was not as big as it is today. At that time, there were not many houses in the neighbourhood behind the Bamenda Provincial Hospital, so he got a good piece of land. By the time of his retirement, houses were on demand. With his pension he had added other rooms and he lived with his tenants as one family.

He love narrating his experiences in the labour room and many lessons could be learnt from him which are not found in any of the textbooks on midwifery. Many of the nurses and midwives visited him when they had the chance. Not only the nurses and midwives visited him but also many other people who found his amiability and the sweet palm wine he always provided a welcome accompaniment to the conversation. It was to him that Russell went to carry out the task which his friend had assigned to him. Russell had to be discreet in his search. He had once accompanied a friend to Pa Nchu's house. He remembered that Pa's endless tales were most of the time about Victoria in those days. He had realized that this was the man to give him the information he needed.

One evening he visited Pa Nchu. Pa recognized Russell as soon as he greeted him.

"You once came here with Neba who works at the Treasury."

"Yes Pa. You have a good memory."

"Yes my son. I thank God for that. I went to school as an adult. Our days were not like today when children who have not left their mother's breast are going to school. It was my good memory that helped me to do the things I did."

They were sitting on his veranda and after this initial conversation Pa waited for Russell to say what had made him visit. Russell was not a worker in his field and Pa knew that the young man must have something serious on his mind. But Pa was not the one to allow the silence to drag on for long when he had so much to talk about to anybody who had the time to come and visit him. As he kept Russell amused with his anecdotes, Pa discreetly posed questions about the young man himself. As Russell listened he thought of how to introduce the topic of Elise's parentage. During a lull in the conversation, Russell began.

"Pa, there is something worrying me. Since I was last here with Mr. Neba, I have realized that you are the only one who can help me." Pa Nchu watched Russell closely, his hands folded on his lap and an encouraging smile on his lips. He was familiar with such beginnings but could not anticipate what was coming after.

"Your knowledge of Victoria and the length of time you have spent there convince me that you must have known this family. There is this nurse in the hospital, Elise Ebende. I have a friend who is interested in her, not just in the way young men do nowadays. But she is so secretive about her family. She says she is an orphan but she must have had uncles and aunts." Pa

106

Nchu's heart was glowing. "Love affairs," he thought. Young people hardly confided their love affairs to him though he enjoyed the intrigues of lovers and would have loved to mediate and see two lovers reunited. In this situation, he wanted to know how far Russell was involved before saying anything. Many people had come to him hiding their problems behind others. He looked Russell straight in the eyes.

"My son, if you are interested in this girl, say so. Do not say that it is your friend." Pa had to be careful. He did not know to what purpose his information was going to be put.

"I am doing this on behalf of my friend who is in Yaounde." He went on to narrate how Elise and Ralph had met and what had resulted from their meeting. The name Ebende was familiar and a common one among the Bakweri people. He had to be careful of what he was about to say.

"I know of one Mr. Ebende who was foreman at the C.D.C. camp near the Bota Hospital. One of his daughters, in fact the eldest one, died after giving birth. There was so much trouble in the family when this woman died." Pa relapsed into a state of reminiscence. "I remember her...such a beautiful woman. I cannot remember her name, but I think she gave birth to a female child. There was another Mr. Ebende but he lived in Mutengene."

This had set Russell thinking. A week later, he visited Elise. While they were talking, he went through her books lying on the table in an assumed absentmindedness. After that he nonchalantly flipped through a file. On the rear jacket of the file was a fold and in this he saw what he was looking for. Her identity card was tucked into this fold. He pulled it out. At this moment, Elise's back was turned to him. He read the names written on it and tried to memorize them. As he did so what caught his attention was this:

Mother's name: Anne Ebende. (Late)
Profession: Teacher
Father's Name: Ebenezer Ebende
Profession: Foreman C.D.C. Bota

He quickly closed the file. He had gotten what he was looking for. The father's profession tied up with what Pa Nchu had told him. Mr. Ebenezer Ebende must be Elise's grandfather not her father. That night he wrote a long letter to Ralph telling him all he had found out and drawing his own conclusions. He tried to be as neutral as he could in the letter. The tone of the letter was one of a trusted friend to another. He did not allow how he felt to be reflected in the letter. But deep down he had a feeling things were not going to work out as his friend was expecting.

It was two weeks now since Ralph had sent the letter proposing marriage to Elise. During the first week he had questioned the rational of his action like someone on trial. There were times he found himself justified in every way. At other times, he was not so sure about the outcome of his action and this opened the door for doubts. As the days came and went, the doubts increased. But they were not enough for him to regret what he had done. Elise had not replied to his letter, but he was prepared to give her time to think about it. The last time he was with her, he had witnessed the level of her insecurity. But he was certain of her love for him.

In this preoccupied mood, his reaction to Claudette's presence became more and more impassive. His mother's constant insinuations were getting on his nerves and he longed for the time to come when he would be financially and physically independent of his mother. He had promised to assist his mother financially with his salary for three months. He had to show some concern for his mother and prop her up in her business before becoming independent.

It was at the beginning of the third week that he received the long awaited letter from Russell. He read through the letter in the office. After work as he lay on his bed, he read the letter again. Certain aspects of it launched him into retrospection. The name Anne Ebende the fact that Elise's biological father was in the United States, the fact that her mother had died after giving birth to her, the fact that the mother was believed to have been killed by a relative of the father. All this made him ill at ease. He ruminated on these facts the whole night. Something at the back of his mind kept nagging at him. He had a fitful sleep filled with nightmares he could not remember the morning. While he was getting his bath the next morning, he soaked his head in the cold

108

spray of water to clear it of the headache that had built up during the night. An idea struck him and the jigsaw puzzle started falling into place.

He remembered that when he was about eight years old there had been talk about his Uncle Andre getting married to a woman called Anne. As he thought about this, the picture of Elise and his uncle flashed through his mind. For the first time, the resemblance struck him. He also remembered snatches of conversation he had overheard that suggested that the whole family was against the marriage. As he stirred the pond of his subconscious, the events became more significant. The information furnished by Russell was tying up with events of the past. He also remembered the day he had witnessed his Uncle Andre quarrelling with his mother. He had just come back from school and there was this scene in the sitting room. He could remember clearly that his uncle was accusing his mother of killing his wife. He had been so hungry that afternoon that he did not wait to hear the rest of what they were saying. He could remember the expression on his mother's face. It was not one of contrition but one of satisfaction. Her words had gone to confirm this. The more Ralph thought about this incident the more his misgivings increased. If all these events were related, he wondered where he stood in all of it. He could not bear to lose Elise. He comforted himself with the fact that they may not be related but he was going to find out.

The Ralph who sat in the office that afternoon was not the Ralph his friend had come to know. He was moody and did not seem to hear what was said to him. Each time he was asked what was wrong he put on a façade of a smile and said he was not feeling fine. He prayed for the first shift of work for the day to be over. At eleven o'clock he left the office explaining to his boss that he was not well and would not be coming back to the office.

That afternoon he turned and tossed on his bed. His thoughts would not allow him to sleep. He picked up a magazine by his bedside and tried to read himself to sleep. He could not concentrate. He put a cassette in the player by his bedside. The record that came on was the one that had been playing on the radio the afternoon he had spent in Elise's house.

109

He turned it off. It aggravated his mental anguish. He did not know when he fell asleep. He got up to find his room dark and came out blinking and protecting his eyes from the glare of the electric bulb.

It was six forty-five in the evening. Sam had already set supper on the table and gone to his lodging two blocks away. His mother was sitting in the parlour with her legs resting on a side stool listening to the radio and waiting for him to get up for them to take supper together. At the sound of his approach, she slowly lifted her eyes and looked at him as he came to sit opposite her.

"You have been sleeping the whole afternoon. What is wrong that you could not even go back to work?" She asked in a concerned tone. Ralph was particularly disorientated by her concern because of the burden he carried within him. He wanted to find out certain things from his mother and he had the impression that the scene was not going to be a pleasant one. He did not respond to his mother's question. She continued, "Let us eat before the food gets too cold." The way Ralph looked at her had made her to decide to leave him alone with his thoughts. If he wanted to talk to her he was free to do so but she was not going to prompt him.

Ralph himself was not conscious of the expression on his face and his mother's silence as they ate, which made him better prepared for what he was about to ask her. As they ate each was preoccupied with different thoughts. Ralph did not know that his mother also had something serious to discuss with him. Whoever began first was going to break the defences of the other. The meal was over and they were still facing each other across the sitting room table.

"Mother, I have something to ask you." Her heart fluttered, hoping it was about Claudette or some other girl he was interested in. "Mother I want you to tell me the truth about what I am going to ask you,." he continued. "Why did father leave you?" This came as a bomb. She had not expected this and was not ready for it.

"Ralph, I think I have answered that question many times."

"Yes, mother. But why did he not take us along with him. When he was settled in Canada, why did he not ask us to join him? It is more than fifteen years since he left. Does he know he has a son like me?"

"Ralph, these questions will lead us nowhere. Have I not brought you up successfully?"

"That is not the point. Look mother, I am an adult now and must know the truth. I better know it from you rather than from another person." .

Madam Essin's temperature was rising as well as her anger. How dare this child question her like that? He was reopening memories she preferred forgotten.

"You do not have to question me like that. You are my child."

"Yes mother, and you have the obligation to tell me the truth. If you don't then you are hiding something from me and whatever it is you are to blame."

"What Ralph! You dare say that to me?"

"Look at me mother. I am no longer a child you can lie to." Madam Essin was defeated and she heaved a sigh. She decided to remain cool. Ralph continued, "That is not all. Can you tell me what happened to the woman uncle Andre was supposed to marry?"

"What!" She jumped from her seat. She could no longer control herself. "Should I know what happened to her? What was my concern about whom he married?" she asked.

"You were opposed to the marriage and did everything to make sure it did not work."

"I had nothing to do with it!" she shouted back at him and started to walk away to her room.

"Yes you killed her." Ralph said this in such a low tone that she did not believe she had heard properly. She stopped in her tracks and turned to him.

"What did you say?"

"It was believed that you killed her." This was too much for her to bear. She felt for the nearest chair and sank into it staring unbelievably at her son. She was deprived of speech.

"The woman's name was Anne Ebende," Ralph continued. "Does that name mean anything to you?"

111

Madam Essin burst into tears. Ralph could not stop. He had to get this out of his system. "She gave birth to a baby girl before she died. Do you know where the baby is? She is the nurse who took care of me at the Bamenda General Hospital."

At the mention of this Madam Essin was shocked and her tears momentarily dried from her eyes. She remembered the resemblance.

"It cannot be true!" she shrieked.

"Yes, it is true. She is the offspring of the love you destroyed." Ralph was becoming hysterical. "Their love was pure and rare. She is a child born of love. That is why she could take so much care of me, a complete stranger. She did all she could for me without complaining. I fell in love with her and wanted to marry her. My love now is my sister. You see how fate works? The clock has wound back to you not to me. I have lost my love but I have a sister worth a thousand lovers. You may wonder how I got to know all this. I asked my friend Russell to find out about her background. I also remember bits of conversations I heard when I was a child. I also remember the day I came back from school and found you and Uncle Andre quarrelling. Your reactions just now confirm all. Do they not? Now I cannot marry Elise, but I will not even consider your Claudette. Goodnight mother."

Madam Essin sat like a statue staring ahead of her. Events had overtaken her. The past had caught up with her. She felt empty, hollow of emotions. She wished for the world to end as she sat there. In fact her world was at a standstill but her conflicting emotions raged like a whirlwind. Her consciousness froze. But she could not remain in this state forever, for nature asserts itself. She suddenly felt hungry. It seemed as if she had not eaten that evening. But how could she eat with so much whirling in her head? She assessed her situation and tried to vindicate herself.

Information about Andre's interest in Anne had gotten to the family when there was this crisis. Perpetua's husband, who had left for Canada after several attempts by the family to reconcile them, had finally sent her divorce papers. The family did not believe that he would go to this extent. They thought that with time he was going to send for his family. She was determined to talk it over with her husband and attempt reconciliation. She was ready to raise money for her plane ticket if he only permitted her to join him so they could try again in a different environment. His replies were not encouraging and she was wise enough to see the futility in trying to go to him without his consent. She calculated the amount of money she would need for her flight and knew it would all be wasted. He had left her with some money and she was yet to decide what to do with her life. Soon other possibilities started finding their way into her head. He could not have asked for divorce if he had not gotten another woman to marry. He had left when Ralph was eight years old and two years later his letters had ceased to come. Then there was the final break. The family was still considering what to do as Perpetua called down fire and brimstone on her husband. The family was still harbouring the bitterness when they received news of Andre's own betrayal and Perpetua took it personally.

After signing the divorce papers and accepting the terms Perpetua had settled down to arranging her life. Business was what appealed to her and she got involved in it with a passion. She had seen her son through secondary school, high school, and university. She had been both mother and father to him. He was the only person around whom her world rotated and now this rejection. It was tearing her apart. As she sat on the chair memories came chasing each other across her mind. She remembered Anne, such a beautiful woman. She had not felt any remorse when she had heard of her death but now she pitied herself. There was not a single reason she could find to vindicate herself. The turn of events had overtaken her.

Granting of leave to hospital staff is not an easy thing. The demand for the work is great. How can you ask to go on leave when you know your section has far more patients than it can handle?

On the other hand, how can you go on leave when there is no definite plan on how you are going to spend the thirty days? Without something definite to do, the boredom of inactivity would push you back to work just to get away from home. Elise had asked for leave but it had not yet been granted. After working for four years without leave she thought this was the right time to do so, so that she could sort out her thoughts. Many things had happened in so short a time. She had planned to spend some days of her leave in Yaounde with Ralph. She really wanted to be with him to find out for herself if what her aunt had told her was true. She never thought of going to her father. Each time she thought of him, a feeling of uncertainty overwhelmed her. She felt safer with the people she knew. Although she had replied to her father's letter, she could not remember how she felt after she had posted the letter. She could not imagine how her father was going to react to the letter. For now that was not her major preoccupation. In the present deadlock with Ralph she wanted a way out. But where would she escape? On whose shoulder would she weep? On Ralph's? Weep on his shoulders as who? Lover or sister? She could not go to aunt Pauline either. Elise could not believe her aunt had known all that and had never told her. She felt it was her right as an adult to know about her background.

The next day Elise dug into her box and brought out the letter her father had written to her. She read it again. This time she did not look on him as a stranger but as a lonely soul reaching out for another. She wept. This time she wept not only for herself but for her mother and father as well. Her mind was no longer in a blur but gradually moving to the light of decision. She withdrew into a world of her own, going about her decision with a single mindedness of purpose that was at once both valuable in its intensity and destructive in its blindness. She believed that this was the time to depend and dwell on herself. She was going to dwell on that self which the world did not know. She was going to depend on that inner strength that pushes people to take decisions that awe them later. The telephone number was quickly scribbled on a piece of paper. On the way to the telephone exchange, Elise was void of emotions. There was not doubt in her mind to make her desist from her action, nor an elated thought to push her forward. She was just a piece of matter in the whirlwind of fate. When the receiver was picked up at the other end, there suddenly appeared a lump in her throat obstructing speech.

"Hello! Hello!" The voice at the other end responded to the ringing of the phone. How was she to begin? What was she to say? The desire to make her father know that she was the one rescued her.

"I am Elise Ebende..." There was a relapse. She struggled to think of what to say next. But the voice at the other end did not give her the chance to continue.

"Elise! My Elise! At last! Let me hear your voice again." She was surprised at the outburst.

"Yes father, I am the one."

"Oh my Elise! My Elise!"

There was some noise at the other end of the line, which she could not determine. The voice when it had called her name sounded tearful. The line seemed to have connected not only their voices but also their emotions and souls. Her eyes were laden with tears and they trickled over. The voice came over again but this time more controlled."

"Elise, I want to see you. I want you to be near me. I love you." There was so much that he wanted to tell her but not over the phone. She too longed to see the face that belonged to that voice. She wanted to see the only person in the world who had the closest blood relationship with her. He continued.

"I will send you an air ticket with the necessary documents for you to come." He checked himself. There had been no response to his enthusiasm. He stopped.

"Elise?"

"Yes father..."

This response brought out all the love he had harboured through the years and which he would have lavished on her. The voice at the other end was choking as it faded off. The lump in her throat was becoming painful, and she fought with it, preventing it from overcoming her. In a strained voice she vented all the emotions of the years gone by.

"Father! Father! I want to see you...be with you..." Andre was in control of himself now and put all earnestness in his voice.

"Elise, I love you. I want you to know that I love you...just as I loved your mother...I want you to be with me...Elise..." Each time he called her name, Anne's picture flashed through his mind and he felt like choking.

"Yes father, I understand. I know that you love me and I know that you loved my mother even more..."

It was a busy week for Elise. Her application for leave was being considered. The director had to make sure that there were enough staff available before he could approve her application. It was a tedious and risky situation for the hospital to be short of staff. Elise could not contend with just waiting. She decided to go and see the director. If it meant losing her job, she was ready to do so just to see her father. When she explained that she intended to spend her leave out of the country, the director had looked at her for a while. He did not want her to notice his surprise so he lowered his gaze and shuffled some papers on his desk. He did not know how to ask about her family. He had got reports about this nurse who did her work and never complained. He had first noticed her when she had volunteered to stay back and help evacuate and attend to the casualties who had been brought in one afternoon after a ghastly motor accident. She had put up the drip sets with such dexterity that the whole exercise looked simple. Here was the time to appreciate what she had done that afternoon but he did not want her to know why he was doing it.

"You can come for your decision in two days."

"Thank you sir," she replied. She could not believe her luck. The joy that had diffused in her body after her conversation with her father increased in intensity. Things were going to work out well she reminded herself. The world was not such a grim place after all. At the Immigration office she did not know what name to give. Her identity card and all her documents bore the name Ebende that took the place of her father's name. Now that she had a father, she wanted to bear his name. The name Kemangou had been written on the letter she had received from her father but she could not use it now because this name was not found on any of her documents. So she made her passport using the names found on her documents. With the passport in the process of being produced, she telephoned and told her father what she had done. He asked for some information and asked her to leave everything in his hands. Two days later she got her leave decision but she did not leave for Yaounde. She did not want to miss whatever mail her father was going to send to her. While she waited, there was this tightness in her stomach, which kept away the appetite for food. On her first day of leave she did not know what to do with herself. This was her first leave in four years and being used to a daily routine she was bored already. She went to the hospital to check for her mails, but there was nothing for her. The following day she decided to visit Russell in his office. She had never been there before and wanted to surprise him. Russell was seated at a table writing. He shared the room with two other men. Since he was used to people entering and leaving the office he did not lift up his head when Elise came in.

"Good morning, Russell." He looked up.

"Ah Elise, you look so...well let me not complete it." They both laughed.

"How is it? It is nice for you to come and see me. How is your work? Is it your day off today?"

"No, I am on leave. It started three days ago."

"That is good. You will have time to rest and make some visits." He winked as he said this and continued, "I am sure that Ralph has written to you."

"Yes he has but I have not yet replied. I do not intend to write."

"Why?" Russell asked in surprise.

"I am going to Yaounde. So there is no need to write"

Ralph had written to tell his friend what he had done. Russell was confused because the expression on Elise's face when she said she was going to Yaounde showed that all was not well.

"I can see that there is something wrong Elise. What is it?" Elise did not realize that Russell had noticed the momentary uncertainty that had fleeted across her face. She brightened up.

"No Russell, there is nothing wrong. When I get there I will look for him."

Russell had thought that her journey to Yaounde was because of Ralph but the tone of her voice indicated the contrary. Russell was now not only surprised but intrigued as to

117

what must have happened after she received the letter. He had expected her to be excited but her tone was matter-of-fact. Russell did not want to go into finding out what had happened. The office was not the appropriate place to find out. So he changed the topic.

"Where else are you going to spend your leave? I am sure you will go to Buea."

"No..." she answered before remembering that she did not want to tell anybody what she was planning to do.

"Well, I will go to Buea, but it all depends..." She stopped.

"Yes it depends," Russell concluded. He knew that much depended on the outcome of her visit to Yaounde. They talked on irrelevances for a while and she got up to go. Russell wanted to probe further to know the real state of affairs. Once they were out of the office he asked.

"When are you leaving for Yaounde? Maybe I should telephone and tell him you are coming."

"I am not certain as yet. But if everything moves well, I will leave before the end of the week."

"Please let me know before you leave. I want to send a letter to Ralph." Elise accepted to inform him but knew she would not. "Okay, see you before you leave."

That afternoon Elise took stock of recent events and decisions in her life. She thought she had made up her mind and there was no turning back, yet deep down uncertainty still lurked. What worried her most was how she was going to face Ralph with the truth she now knew. She also thought of her leaving everybody she knew for a strange place and to live with a man who claimed to be her father. The only sure thing she knew about him was his voice. She kept imagining what her life would look like living with Ralph as his wife. Then she thought of living in America with her father. The idea of going to America appealed to her. The thought of going to meet her father also appealed to her. But between the dream and the reality questions were lined up. What was she going to do with her professional knowledge? Would she continue to work as a nurse? She had heard that nurses were in demand, so on that she was not worried. What was her aunt going to do and say when she received the letter she was planning to write? She had taken the decision unilaterally. She thought of her aunt's reaction but was consoled by the fact that by the time she receives the letter the damage would have been done. Moreover, she would not be around to be a witness to the consequences. She thought about Ralph, his love for her and her love for him. The fact that she had a blood relationship with him was still unreal, for she still loved him as a woman loves a man. If it was true and if she remained in Cameroon, what would she do? Would this love suddenly cease?

For the next few days her thoughts dwelled on the impending journey. She did not know what to do with herself for the time to pass faster, while she waited for the documents her father had promised to send. Not being used to lying in bed till late in the morning Elise got up each morning and kept herself busy washing and cleaning both in and around her house. One morning she decided to go to the hospital and visit her colleagues and some patients she had admitted. As she passed by the nurses' station with the intention of visiting the patients first, one of the nurses called for her and pressed a piece of paper into her hand. It was a receipt requesting her to come to the Post office and collect a parcel. With a beating heart she read the words on the sheet of paper. She was so happy that she momentarily forgot she was standing with her colleagues.

"Go and get it quickly. But do not forget to bring our share," one of the nurses shouted after her as they walked away leaving her still looking at the sheet of paper. Every document had been signed at the Cameroonian Embassy in the United States. All she had to do was get a visa and apply for leave from the governor indicating that she wanted to spend her holidays in America. In an accompanying letter, her father explained that this was all formality. Included in the parcel was a cheque of five hundred dollars, which the bank would change for her into traveller's cheques. When she checked to see when her flight was scheduled, she realized that she had barely a week to get herself ready. There was no turning back. She started cleaning up in earnest. She packed all the dresses she was going to leave behind into her valise. All her books were packed into two

119

cartons. While she packed she realized that one never knows how much a room can contain until you start getting the things together. Her chairs and bed were left as they were. Her aunt would collect them. Her plan was mapped out but her actions and reactions to the situations she was going to face could not be mapped out.

The last thing she did was telephone her secondary school classmate and friend who had gone to the university and was now working in the Ministry of Finance and tell her about her impending journey to Yaounde. Her dreams during the nights of these days were full of fantasia. With the cheque in her bag and the documents in a file she was ready to take the first step that was going to open the way for her.

Russell had telephoned Ralph telling him about Elise's impending journey to Yaounde. She had not been specific about her day of departure because she did not want Ralph to wait for her and monopolize her. If this happens, then she would not have enough time with her friend to catch up on what they would say to each other. Moreover Elise knew that she was going to face a difficult situation and wanted to have someone on whom she could rely. Before meeting Ralph, she wanted to tell Rita all that had happened.

As soon as Ralph got the message of Elise's impending journey to Yaounde, he hurried with the arrangements he had been making to move into his own apartment. He had planned to get into it even if there was only a bed in it. He wanted to have Elise to himself. He wanted to be alone with her before she met his mother. And this would not be possible if he was still in his mother's house.

Since the exchange between mother and son, Madam Essin realized that to continue to be angry with her son would further estrange him from her. She was ready to do everything to bridge the gap. Ralph did not mind her efforts, for he too could not stand the strained atmosphere. He had given her three quarters of his first salary. This had gladdened her heart and she was reassured that her son would never abandon her. Ralph had intended doing the same with his second salary but with the turn of events he needed money to set himself up. When Ralph

120

told his mother he wanted to move into a place of his own earlier than he had planned, his mother's doubts started again. When she offered to equip the apartment for him he declined, insisting that he was a man now and wanted to do things his own way and at his own pace. He got the apartment and bought a bed. He also got a mattress and bed sheets. He bought blinds and put them on the two windows.

8

hree days to the day that Russell had suggested Elise would come to Yaounde, Ralph started making trips to the Carrefour Obili bus stop very afternoon. His first two trips were unsuccessful, but on the third day he was about to go away again disappointed when he saw a bus loaded with bags of Irish potatoes and cabbages coming into the bus stop. These two food items were indicative of where the bus was coming from. It was certain that it was either from the North West Province or the Western Province. He waited hoping Elise would be on the bus. And she was. She came out of the bus but concentrated on waiting for her valise to be brought down. She had heard of thieves making away with people's luggage from this bus stop and did not want to be a victim. This gave Ralph enough time to get near to her without her noticing his approach. She was so occupied looking up at the carriage of the bus that she did not realize that someone was standing beside her. When the valise got to the level of her hands, another pair of hands came up to assist her. She thought it was one of the park boys helping her. When she looked up to see who it was and to thank the person, her eyes met with Ralph's. He had on that disarming smile. She was not prepared for such a reception and did not know what to do or say. The convention of logic and reason had no place in her mind at that moment. She was carried away by a momentary impulse. When the valise was brought down and kept on the ground, she fell into his arms. He held her close while his heart pulsated within him. There was no desire for speech but the passing of time forced them to it.

"Elise, I have missed you so much."

"So have I," she replied.

She wanted to ask him how he knew when she would be coming, but decided that it was not an appropriate question to ask considering the circumstances. Each of them was behaving as if everything was all right. Each thought of what the revelation would do to the other.

"I am staying not far from here with a friend. She gave me the directions to her house," Elise informed him to preempt any offer on his part. She continued, "You know I don't know the town well. I hope you won't mind accompanying me there."

"Sure Elise. You know that I am ready to go anywhere with you." He sounded like the Ralph she had known as a patient and the thought made her smile. He saw her smile and was pleased about it. They left the bus stop and waited for a taxi by the roadside. Elise looked so natural in her every word and action that Ralph's heart constricted with apprehension when he thought of how she would react to what he had come to learn.

When they arrived at their destination in the Biyamassi neighbourhood, fortunately her friend Rita was home. They were so excited to see each other that they forgot about Ralph's presence. Even when they were in the house and seated, they continued to talk as if Ralph was not there. Ralph watched them and was amused and admired their simple joy at seeing each other. Underneath her joy, Elise wondered how she was going to explain Ralph's presence. After the euphoria of the meeting was over, Elise turned to Ralph, looked at him for a moment then she turned to Rita.

"Rita, please meet Ralph. I have been so rude not to introduce him earlier. I am sure it was the excitement of seeing you. Ralph, I am sorry for not introducing my friend to you earlier. I hope both of you are going to forgive me. I am just so happy to be here." Ralph believed Elise's happiness had to do with him and for a moment he pushed aside all knowledge of the possibility of their being related. He looked at his watch and realized he was already late for the afternoon shift of work and needed to go. But he could not go without speaking to Elise first. He excused himself and moved out with the knowledge that Elise was going to accompany him outside and he would use this opportunity to speak to her. He had this feeling of excitement tinged with dread. He was finding it difficult to make an about turn in his feelings for her but he had to face whatever the future had in store for them. Elise was in Yaounde. There was no escape.

He convinced himself that Elise could not be his sister in the African sense of the word. He had never really imagined how he could have reacted to a sister. In his childhood, from the way his friends treated their sisters, he had had the impression that they were a nuisance. They were never allowed to play football with them. He wished he had had a sister like Elise. He would have liked to play with her all the time. But Ralph was not a small boy. He was a man and the way he wanted to be close with Elise was not like a brother wanting to be with a sister. He felt something stronger for her.

He wanted her to meet his mother. He wanted this whole matter to be sorted out. If it were a misunderstanding, which he hoped it was, he longed for it to be cleared off as soon as possible. But first he had to tell her what he had learnt form Russell. This was the difficult part.

That night Elise lay conversing with Rita in her two-bedroom studio. She could no longer hide why she was in Yaounde. As she talked about going to the United States to meet her father, she really felt an unmingled joy for the first time. The prospect of living a new life, seeing new places and in fact meeting her father became more real. She even felt grateful, considering the information she had to tell Ralph. It was a good way of separating. Out of sight out of mind. But she never mentioned anything about Ralph.

Rita was so interested in the turn of events that she questioned Elise about her family while she fitted in bits of information she had heard when they were in the primary and secondary schools. The subject of Elise's parentage had been a sore spot and as friends, Rita had avoided telling her what she had heard about Elise's mother. But now the coast was clear for her to say some of them.

"I heard that your father's people did not want the marriage."

"That I know."

"How did you know?"

"I got to know recently. But that was in the past. I want to look forward. My father wants me now. That is what is important."

Rita even felt a bit jealous that Elise was about to go to America. The idea of going to America has always been a dream to young people. Rita's curiosity was not satisfied. She had learnt so much since Elise came to her. She wanted to get to the bottom of it all. But Elise's response had showed that there was no use continuing on the topic. She turned to Elise, "Forgive me if I have been inquisitive."

On the subject of Ralph, Elise was evasive. What was she to say after all? Who was Ralph to her now? She had not even told Ralph what her aunt had told her. So for the moment as far as things stood between the two of them they were about to be engaged. But this Rita was never to know. Before Elise fell asleep, she resigned herself to the fact that what had happened had happened and what had to happen would happen. She would go on living. Life was not going to come to a standstill.

They next day Rita left Elise in bed when she went to work. Elise enjoyed the feeling of having nothing to do and just being by herself. She had been used to working or keeping herself busy by doing one thing or the other. It had never occurred to her that she would give herself the novelty of lying in bed and doing nothing. The prospect of beginning a new life enthralled her and she wanted to enjoy the feeling. She had grown up with the belief that for her to succeed in life she had to work hard. Lying in bed on a working day morning was a sign of laziness. But this morning she could afford to be lazy. With Rita's help she was going to call the embassy and book for an interview. She had all the required documents. She had cashed the cheque and changed some of the money into Cameroonian currency. It was so much money. She had never had so much money on her at one time. The bundle of notes had been separated and hidden in three different parts of her valise. When Rita came back from work she and Elise went to town. Rita wanted to show her friend the town. They took a taxi to Marche Central and looked around. There was nothing that Elise wanted to buy in particular. They sampled the prices of some items which they had no intention of buying. Elise was amazed at the variety of second hand goods for sale and their prices. Rita wanted to do the best for her friend. She wanted to give Elise a nice time. She had thought that Elise would be excited to buy some of the things they saw at the shops. But she was disappointed. Elise had always been secretive but as an adult now Rita thought she had changed. She had been equally surprised that Elise had not talked about any boyfriend. But she had noticed the way Ralph had looked at Elise. Her evasive answers whenever Ralph was mentioned made her think there was something going on.

As they moved around her mind kept going round to Ralph. She knew he was going to come to look for her in the afternoon and was partly grateful that they were out. After Ralph had left the previous day she had not told Rita about him except to say he was just a friend who had offered to accompany her to make sure she got to her destination safely. She prayed that Rita should not ask her about Ralph again. And she did not. Elise was tired from the visit to the market. On their way back they had had to stand for almost thirty minutes before getting a taxi to get them home.

The next morning, Rita had gone to work. Elise was alone in the house. There was really nothing for her to do. Everything for her journey was almost ready. She had been packed since Bamenda and she was booked for her interview the next day. After a long period of meditating on how to tell her aunt the decision she had taken she decided to write her a letter. It was a tedious letter. She wanted to be fair with herself as well as her aunt. It was not a means of vindicating herself or rationalizing her decision, but she wanted to call a spade a spade. She also knew that no matter what she said her aunt would be hurt. She tried to make the impact of her letter less painful by assuring her aunt that she would never forget her and calling on her to try and understand the situation in which she found herself. She started by expressing appreciation for what her aunt had done for her. After reflecting on this she tore it up. How could she express appreciation as if it was a contract that had been well carried out? She had sucked at her breasts. She had taken her as her mother and all the feeling she had for a mother had been directed towards her. When she thought about Ralph she became more confused. What was she to tell her aunt? She wondered. Then she decided to leave any mention of Ralph and his proposal out of the letter. Her going to her father was confirmation of the story her aunt had told her and it was evident enough that she was not going to marry Ralph, so there was no need to mention it. Before she fell into another restless sleep she was satisfied with what she had written. It was a letter that had the semblance of a heart's outpouring but underneath there was some reticence, which stemmed from a desire to begin the process of separation. With the letter written she had the next problem to solve. She had not yet told Ralph the two things that were going to separate though unite them.

A knock at the door woke her up with a start. Each time she slept in a strange place she always got up with this sense of not knowing where she was. Her short sleep had been full of fantasia flowing backwards and forward. Scenes from the past mingled with those of the present and the future. Her sleep was the type that leaves you feeling tired instead of refreshed. From the manner of knocking she knew that it was her friend Rita. She got up and opened the door.

"You look tired Elise," Rita remarked.

"I have been sleeping."

"On the contrary, you should not look as tired. Sleep is supposed to take away tiredness not generate it."

"I did not know what to do with myself this morning so I fell asleep. I do not usually sleep in the mornings. That may be why."

"I hope that you are not too tired to go to town with me. Our directors and sub directors are having a meeting and there is not much work in the office so I decided to come and take you out."

"That is a good way of spending the afternoon. I was just imagining how I was going to sit here alone all afternoon."

"What about the man who came with you the day you arrived. Who is he Elise? Do not hide anything from me."

"You mean Ralph? He must be at work. Maybe he will call in the evening." Rita could not control her curiosity about the man. She had found him very handsome and would have liked to know more about him. Plus Elise's reservations had intrigued her. She had to say something to open up the subject.

"Where does he work?"

"I think he works at the Ministry of Finance."

"Then I have not seen him?"

"I am not very sure about that but it has not been long since he started work. Maybe he is not in the same section as you."

Elise was evasive in her answer and did not want the conversation to continue. It might make her say things she did not want to reveal. The hesitation in her voice made Rita stop her trend of questions but was she not convinced by Elise's answer and made a mental note to find out.

The shops were filled with items Elise had longed for. With the amount of money she had she could have bought many. But she wondered what she would do with them since she was in transit. More so, her father had told her not to bother about bringing many dresses. She also had that panic reflex about money common in those brought up without enough of it. She had been brought up to be contented with the little she had.

Ralph came for her that evening. She could not say that she expected him to visit her or that she dreaded his visit. Everything was so mixed up in her mind. She did not in her heart of hearts accept the turn fate had taken on her. She still loved Ralph although she knew it was going to lead to nothing. She had to accept the fact that he was her cousin as the white men would put it but for now this conversion had not yet taken place. There were times that she ruminated on the moments of communion they had shared together. She lingered on them awhile trying to recapture the pleasure that had coursed through the liquid surf of her blood pulsating against the inner cliffs of her heart. These thoughts momentarily brought a smile to her lips. This was momentary because the passing of the days and the force of events were pushing her ahead.

They found themselves alone again after a long time and after so much had taken place. There was a table and two chairs in the parlour. Apart from a shelf containing some books that he had brought from his mother's house the room was bare. They sat on the chairs and did not speak for some time. The air around them was charged with the emotional tension that filled them and overflowed through their eyes, breath and clammy palms. She looked at his profile, his strong jaws and sensuous mouth and imagined how she would have felt if she had gone to bed with him. The thrill of the experience brought a smile to her lips.

She thought of how it would feel to lie side by side with him. Imagination at that point was a piece of luggage she could not afford to carry so she abandoned it for more concrete things. Ralph's words cut into her thoughts.

"Elise, we have to face this together. We have to act as support for each other. What I am going to tell you is going to hurt you. I have no choice but to let you know the truth..." He was finding it difficult to say what he had to say. It was also heavy in his chest. He continued, "The point is...I learnt not long ago that..."

"Stop," Elise whispered. "I know. You do not need to tell me..."

All evening she had been trying to control herself but now she gave up and allowed the tears to flow. He held her close and heaved a sigh of relief.

"Oh Ralph! Ralph! Why should this happen? Why! Why! You are the first man that I have loved this way. Just when I thought I had found my partner in life I am thrown out again..." she sobbed. "What have I really done lord! That at my age I should suffer so much?"

Her present suffering was the loss of a person she had nursed and cherished in her heart to fill the vacuum in her existence. A vacuum that was a desire for love and emotional support – one that could not be filled by a well paid job or even an aunt's love. Her feelings were in the doldrums, in the funnel of a tornado where everything is motionless, while the whirlwind of her mind goes round and round.

Ralph on his part while he held her close tried to master this new situation. As he held her the flow of excitement that used to rush down his spine each time he held her gave way to a warm feeling from his heart and a desire to hold her closer and more firmly. There was now in him the desire to protect her from the world. He felt that he could fight any danger that threatened her. All the love he had imagined he could lavish on a kid sister if he had one came coursing through his being and his embrace became more crushing. His efforts were all against no physical danger, for the real danger was intangible. It lay in their hearts and the present situation provoked it further. Her heartbeat increased as he held her closer and closer. The suffocating embrace had not allowed him to speak so that she could know how he felt about the whole situation. His embrace seemed to tell her that he loved her just as before as if nothing had happened and this frightened her. She pulled herself away from him as she wiped away her tears. Ralph stood and looked at her but was not seeing her. He was struggling to make the final break.

"I want you to meet my mother. We have to go and see her."

This was said in such a determined voice that Elise's fright was increased and she stepped back again. In her fright she looked like a scared child. This appealed to Ralph who could not resist taking her into his arms again. In a meditative voice he said, "There is no way she can avoid the relationship between us. She has to face it."

This statement further confirmed her fears. What if Ralph insisted on overlooking the blood relationship that exists between them to go ahead with this idea of marriage? After all nothing had been confirmed yet. It had all been hearsay. What was she going to do now that her mind was made up in a different direction? She could not stand the idea of disappointing him. He had to know the truth of the new developments. For a moment she heard the voice of her father over the phone. She pictured the man with the voice and imagined how her change of mind was going to affect him. What of myself? She suddenly thought. I have myself to consider as well. I have my life to live and whatever becomes of me depends largely on me before those around me. Whatever way events are going to turn out I am going to be related to her in one way or the other. She knew that their meeting with Madam Essin was not going to be a pleasant one and the sooner it was over the better.

The lady had aged considerably since Elise had last seen her. Her eyes betrayed this more than her face. Though the streaks of grey hair on her temple were testimonies of the passing of years, her face with the help of foundation creams and night masks still looked firm. The folds on her neck had reduced, giving the scapula more prominence and the neck a scrawny look. The loss of weight might have given her a youthful appearance but the lack of lustre in her eyes and the slouching posture made her look old. She sat as if she had been sitting there all her life waiting for something to happen but not knowing what. The well groomed woman who had sat in the hospital ward with such opulence and confidence – giving instructions and expecting to be obeyed and trying to make the lives of others satellites of hers – now sat like a chicken stripped of its feathers.

At the hospital Elise had viewed her with awe and avoided her presence because she felt eclipsed by her exuberance. She had that type of effect on people that is produced by the presence of an important personality among ordinary people. Each gesture, each change in tone of voice and even the blinking of her eyelids which made her face so expressive was a masterpiece of an unconscious assertion of her will and ideas on those around her.

Elise stood there trying to seek a compromise between what was and what is. She glanced sideward at Ralph and their eyes met. All this while Madam Essin was looking at Elise. But as Elise moved to her seat neither the gaze nor its direction, nor the expression on Madam Essin's face changed. The young people looked at each other again. The silence was heavy and Ralph involuntarily cleared his throat. This might have seemed as a deliberate attempt to draw attention. Its sudden production and the silence of the room made it sound particularly loud. Madam Essin temporarily looked at her visitors and dropped her gaze. In the split second that her eyes had met with Elise's, she saw all that condemned her. Although the look in her eyes was more of bewilderment than of accusation, the guilt on Madam Essin's conscience blinded her to this and she only saw Elise's face through her guilt. Her guilt was further aggravated by a whole lot of incidents. She was not responsible for Elise's misfortune, but the fact that she had chipped off a piece of masonry from that other edifice of a relationship haunted her in the person of Elise. It was as if three people looked at her through Elise, each in their separate ways accusing her of deprivation…of life, of a daughter, of a mother and a father. And then there was the look of her son, deprived of a lover and of a sister. She was wondering what they had come to do. Had they come to degrade her further? She wondered, for she was sure they now knew the truth. She waited for them to say whatever they had come to say. They were making her face herself and it was a painful process. A process that made her heart ache and took her to the depths of self pity. Her mind was beginning to accept the fact that this was her punishment. And it was one she was ready to accept. From this depth something suddenly leapt at her. What if Ralph had come to tell her that he wanted to marry this girl? She wondered. What was she going to do? She saw her son getting involved in a complicated situation and her blood became warm in her veins. She became very hot.

She rose quickly from the lowly depths of despair and self pity and took a defensive stance. Elise had been watching her closely, especially her eyes. She did not miss the sudden change. The glint that appeared in her eyes changed her countenance. The knitting of her eyebrows and the tightening of her lips indicated that something had changed. Elise's heart raced. She looked from mother to son and back to mother.

"Mother, we have come to see you. I want you to meet Elise Bekayo…" his voice faltered. He turned and looked at Elise. She was looking straight at his mother. He had used this name to hammer home the fact that Elise was no longer a stranger but a member of the family. Andre had been named after his grandfather who was also Madam Essin's father. His introduction trailed off because of the expression he found on Elise's face.

How would a victim react face to face with the supposed cause of his misery? With a strong desire to hit back no matter how feeble the punch? By pouring out a stream of abuses? By putting on a look of scorn thus pretending to live above the situation? No. All these were momentary impulses that leave no lasting results. The sweetest revenge is forgiveness, for it robs the victim of the real reason to despise you. You leave him in a perpetual state of uncertainty, pushing him to misinterpret and be afraid of every little action you take or words you mention. This is the basis of real mental torture. Elise looked at Madam Essin again. Her whole life was believed to have been upset by this woman. At that moment the picture of her mother flashed across her mind's eye. She had looked at this picture innumerable times. It was the one Andre had focused on the first day he had visited her mother. The picture was stamped somewhere in her mind. It seemed to help Elise muster courage. Although Elise felt some relief from some undefined cloud that had hung over her existence, she also felt strongly that there was a way of getting back at Madam Essin without changing her mind. At that moment it seemed as if there was nothing Elise could do apart from looking at Madam Essin. She realized what her Achilles' heel was. If she were to get back at her, she now knew how. Deliberately she drew closer to Ralph and sent her arm round him. His proximity gave her some emotional stability and she looked at Madam Essin as one would look at a dog that had just stolen and eaten a large piece of meat, angry but impotent to do anything at that moment.

9

*M*adam Essin's life was deteriorating before her very eyes. All she had toiled to build was falling apart. This girl and the way she was taunting her conscience were destroying the future she had built for her son and herself. Ralph's return from France had given her more impetus to move ahead and complete her life by making his life part of hers. Her desires had taken a concrete existence in her mind. She had reassured herself time and time again of the success of her hopes to the point that it was impossible for her to distinguish between what was probable and what was not. The meeting with Elise had punched a hole in this once so strong vision. Now it was sagging like a bulky mass of flesh, slopping, bulging again and then falling away in all directions. Just as it was about to fade away from her vision she gripped the last tangible part of it. She held fast to it, trying to recapture the strength of her determination by examining her position in view of the past the present and the future.

Madam Essin did not believe it was fate alone which had brought her to such a situation. But if it were fate what had she done to deserve what she was going through now? She wondered. She had done nothing to harm Anne. All she had done was try to dissuade her from marrying her cousin. She had not hurt her by deeds, only by words. News of her death had shocked her although she had felt no remorse. Her championing of the family's cause was one way of releasing the tension that had built up in her when she had received the last letter from her husband about the divorce. This was the underlying reason for her desire to see that Andre did not marry Anne. She wanted to win the favour of the family by shifting attention from her predicament and putting herself in better light. To the family Andre was making a mistake by marrying Anne. He deserved a wife who was socially and academically better placed than

134

Anne. The family's stand was further buttressed by the fact that Anne was not from the same tribe as they. These were the arguments she had carried with her. But when she had met Anne face to face, her beauty had made Perpetua really jealous. Her cool composure in the face of such taunts and abuses showed that she was the winning type. Perpetua did not like this because it had become a tradition in the family for the females to subdue the women who married into the family. All Perpetua's efforts to look dashing had been met by a look of disinterestedness rather than admiration which she had expected.

These reminiscences left a bitter taste in Madam Essin's mouth. What had she really achieved? She wondered. Looking at the past from the vantage point of maturity, she felt pangs of regret for the first time. Her regret was not for what had happened but for what was happening. The past was past and done with although it had left in its wake a string of problems. With all these thoughts in her mind, Madam Essin decided to channel all her energies towards recuperating her confidence in her vision and working towards it. All was not lost. Furthermore she was not the type of woman to allow herself to be drowned by events. Had she not lived through and overcome more devastating situations? What would hurt more than being abandoned by a husband? Nothing. Not even Ralph's estrangement from her was going to make her give up. After all, he was still her son. She believed that sooner or later he would come to his senses.

All these thoughts had been going through her mind as she sat at her dressing table three days after her meeting with Elise, combing her hair into the desired style. What the mirror showed her was the inescapable present written into the skin of her face, each line of bone, the set of her lips and the tilt of her chin. Acceptance of this picture was acceptance of defeat. She rubbed foundation powder into the creases in her face before applying a light dust of white powder. She liked white powder because it made the skin on her face look younger. She told herself that although Ralph was a grown up man she was not yet an old woman. She still had steam and could stand her ground against any situation she faced. These comforting thoughts swarmed and warmed her features. Her lips tightened with a sudden spasm of resolve. Her chin involuntarily lifted and an uncanny light came into her eyes. She smiled at the woman in the mirror. The woman smiled back. Her confidence was restored as she stepped out of the bedroom.

What drew her attention as she entered the parlour was the silence. She stood for some time absorbing the silence and the impact it was having on her. Ralph's absence from the house had not affected her as it did that morning. All the things she had surrounded herself with and which had acted as a buffer between her and despair now looked at her with equanimity. They no longer produced in her the sense of achievement and success she had always prided herself on. On closer look she discovered that the leather on the upholstered chairs were faded. Her heart had filled out with pride when she had bought these chairs and they were brought into her parlour and put in place. At that time this particular model of chairs were the craze in town and possessing one was not only a sign of wealth but also that of good taste. The whole set was made of three pieces with each piece of three seats made to conveniently fit into an angle of the room. The leather was cream white and with the matching blinds, the set had given her parlour a cheerful look that was exactly how she had felt on that day and many days after. The parlour was a reflection of how far she had gone up the social ladder in spite of the loneliness that often threatened to envelope her especially when she saw a couple moving together or watched them dance at a party. At such moments she used to imagine how it would have been if her husband were still with her.

Now the parlour looked dismal. It was a gloomy morning. The rays of the sun that used to stream in through the blinds creating the effect of suffused lighting were absent. Her eyes shifted to the carpet on the floor. It looked dirty. She then realized that Sam had been too silent since Ralph's departure. She made a mental note to talk to him and find out if he still valued his job or not. The top of the cupboard and the top of the stereo set were dusty. It looked as if the parlour had not been cleaned for days. She could hear him humming a song to himself in the kitchen. Just as she was about to call him and admonish him for his negligence she heard music coming from the direction of Ralph's room. She stood rooted at the spot listening. Yes the music was from his room. Had he stealthily come back? Was he too ashamed to face her? Had he come back to ask for forgiveness for what he had done? These questions warmed her heart as she moved towards the room. At the door she stopped and turned the handle. It opened but the room was empty. Ralph had left without closing the louvers on the windows of his room. The music was coming from her neighbour's parlour, which was separated from the window of Ralph's room by a wire fence. The music from this neighbouring house had always strained their relationship especially when Ralph was occupying the room. On many afternoons he could not sleep because it was so loud. She banged the door with anger not only from her disappointment but also from memories of her recent confrontations with these people. She walked quickly out of the house, forgetting that she wanted to talk to Sam about the state of the parlour. As she walked to the roadside to get a taxi to her shop, she took time to reflect on her thoughts of that morning. She realized that she was not ready to part with Sam. She still needed his services. It was difficult to get house help like Sam.

He did his work well. He was also respectful and never interfered in her life. She did not want to give him the opportunity of giving her notice of his going away. She could see it coming. She had to talk to him, not in the way she had planned but in a sober manner making him see the reason in continuing to stay. Now that Ralph had left she was going to reduce his salary, but it was going to be higher than before.

She arrived at the market at nine o'clock. The other shops were already open. Looking at her closed shop in the row of already bustling shops made her heart flutter. The closed door seemed to bar her from what she was looking forward to. Was this how life was going to be without Ralph? Was it going to be a closed door in the midst of humanity? Was there going to be nothing to indicate that she had been there? The door stood like a barrier to all that she had been longing for. But what it was, she wondered.

Madam Essin walked towards her closed shop as if the minutes were ticking to zero point. Opening the shop and walking in was like getting onto safe ground before danger strikes.

"Good morning Perpetua," her neighbour in the shop opposite hers called out in greeting.

"Good morning," Perpetua replied looking at her briefly so as not to appear rude or give the impression there was something wrong with her. This would be like revealing her predicament and giving them reason to talk about her in her absence. Her lateness made it evident that all was not well with her. In the midst of trouble there is always one person to rely on. Bernadette, the woman who had greeted her moved over to join her.

"You are very late today Perpetua. It is not like you. What happened to keep you at home for so long in the morning?"

The women, being of the same age, were on first name basis. They were birds of a feather and had much more in common than the other shopkeepers on the same row. They were considerably well off but considered their present occupations and even their presence in the market as something not of their making. If they had to choose they would have preferred to be somewhere else. The use of academic achievement to create a psychological barrier has always helped to elevate people's conception of themselves. Madam Essin was a university drop out but she had made herself believe she had a university degree. This was a secret she guarded jealously for very few people knew the truth. But the dream of what she had wanted to be still haunted her and she had done everything to see that this dream was fulfilled in her son. Bernadette was also a university drop out. As they sat and waited for customers to come into their shops they had enough time to bemoan their fate. They did not miss any opportunity to talk about when they were in the university to show the other shopkeepers that they were academically better than they were. Even on this basis, Madam Essin still considered herself better than Bernadette because she could afford to go to Cotonou to buy goods for her shop while Bernadette had never gone out of Yaounde. More to this Madam Essin had always prided herself on her son's successes, achievements and obedience. Revealing the truth now would destroy the image she had created and sustained.

"I overslept because I am not feeling fine. I have just managed to come this morning."

"Where is Marie? If she comes today you can go home. You do not look well at all." Marie was the girl whom Madam Essin called occasionally to assist her in the shop when she had other things to do. Sometimes she came of her own accord when she had time to spare. Madam Essin compensated her handsomely and she never missed any opportunity to come to her assistance.

The other shopkeepers had watched Madam Essin's late arrival with nonchalance. They saw her pass and continued to attend to their customers or do whatever they were doing. Whatever had made her come late was none of their business because she was never interested in other people's problems. She always kept a superior aloofness. Unfortunately for her their long hours of sitting and waiting for customers had made the shopkeepers develop the ability of noticing the unconscious mannerisms people put on to create an impression. From long observations they had seen through Madam Essin. They had seen the vanity of her pretensions and dismissed her from their conversations. But this morning there was something about her to talk about. She had always railed against shopkeepers who came late to their shops. She always believed that the best sales were done in the morning period. But today she herself was late. Whatever happened to her, Madam Essin did not cherish being pitied.

"It is all right. I can manage. I took some medication before coming." As she spoke she rummaged through her handbag not knowing exactly what she was looking for. Bernadette stood for some time looking at her friend. She had come to tell her something but her preoccupation did not give her the chance to do so. As she contemplated what to do she heard the voice of a woman asking if there was somebody in her shop. She rushed out to attend to the woman. This was the third buyer who had walked into her shop that morning. The first two had not bought anything. She now rushed to this one with the

139

hope of making a sale. On second thoughts she did not really care whether she sold that day or not. What was in her heart and which she was dying to tell Perpetua was satisfaction enough.

Madam Essin pulled out the lower drawer of her cupboard. It did not contain what she was looking for. She lifted her handbag to have a look. It was quite heavy. Apart from the compact powder set, perfume, deodorant, lipstick and pocket mirror, which she carried around like ammunition against any eventuality, there was also the small leather bag which contained her bank savings and her post office savings booklets. There were two other smaller booklets, which contained her savings in two other thrift and loan groups. She took out her bank savings booklet first. B.I.C.E.C. was her bank. She had confidence in them. They had given her loans on many occasions. These had financed her many trips to Cotonou and to Abidjan. She flipped through and looked at her deposits and withdrawals for the last two and a half years. On the last page in the balance column was written the sum of five million one hundred and twenty two thousand francs. She smiled with satisfaction then remembered that she had the sum of five hundred thousand francs to pay back to the Business Women's Association. Then she thought of the set of chairs, carpet and matching blinds she was planning to buy for Ralph as a surprise gift when he eventually moved to his own apartment. This would take some one million three hundred thousand francs. She would be left with more than three million francs. That was good enough for now. If Ralph gave her the one hundred thousand francs he had promised to give her every month for the first six months, then she would be able to pay off the loans she had taken for her recent trip to Cotonou. She then took out her post office savings booklet. There was the sum of seven hundred thousand francs written in the balance column. This was to cater for eventualities at home like ill health or an unplanned trip to the village, or even to help one of her numerous relatives in Yaounde.

While she was thus occupied many buyers looked but on seeing her busy passed by without bothering to come in. Potential buyers are encouraged by attention from the shopkeeper. They even have to be cajoled into buying

140

something. Sometimes flattery comes in very handy. But Mrs. Essin did not care whether anything was bought from her shop that morning. Going through her bank records had raised her spirits. She was in a lighter mood. She stood up and absentmindedly started examining the goods she had in her shop. The shop was divided into three sections. Directly opposite the door were shelves with packets of lace materials. Some were unwrapped and displayed. On the left were wrappers of different qualities. There were Holland wax, English wax, Nigerian prints and a selection of Cicam materials. On the right were *boubous* from Cotonou. On a revolving stand near the door she usually had Afritude jumpers for men. The *boubous* and jumpers were the craze in town and their prices ranged from twenty-five thousand francs to seventy-five thousand francs. They were all in plastic sheaths to keep them free from dust. She had brought fifty *boubous* from Cotonou and only eight were left. The Afritude jumpers had all been sold. When women heard that she was back from a trip or had just received a consignment of goods, they flocked to her house to make their choices before she took them to the market. From her sales she had made more than a hundred percent gain. But much of the money was still outstanding because some woman had taken dresses on credit. She was not worried because she knew that whatever happened, she was going to get the money. She touched the material of one of the *boubous* and sighed with contentment. She decided that no matter how long these remained in the shop, she was not going to reduce the price. Psychology plays a big role in business, especially if you are dealing with women. If she reduced the price the quality would go down in the eyes of the woman. They believed that the more expensive a dress is, the higher the quality. So shrewd businesswomen like Madam Essin used this to their advantage. She was busy contemplating her financial gain from her recent trip when Bernadette came in again.

"Perpetua, I have good news which I wanted to tell you when you came in. But I saw that you were not in the mood for conversation."

Madam Essin looked at her friend with a smile on her face ready to share in the good news. Bernadette continued, "Belinda has given birth to a baby boy."

Madam Essin was momentarily speechless. Then she regained herself.

"Congratulations. Congratulations. So you are a grandmother now. Lucky you. We are surely going to celebrate this. When are we going to celebrate?"

"Her husband sent a message asking me to come immediately I get the news. So I am leaving for Douala tomorrow morning. We will celebrate when I come back."

A woman was standing in front of Bernadette's shop wondering whether to go away or walk in and find out if there was anybody in. It was clear from her behaviour that she was from one of the neighbouring villages. These were the women who were sure to make a purchase. Such women did not have the time to come to the market for window shopping. If they came then they wanted something. Bernadette rushed back to her shop. She also sold wrappers but recently she had added ladies' shoes.

Madam Essin sat back and imagined how it felt to be a grandmother, to have a baby to hold and cuddle. She could not remember when she last carried a baby. They always irritated her especially with their persistent cries. But now she longed for one. This sudden desire to carry a baby surprised her. Was it old age that was overtaking her? Was she going downhill already? She looked across at Bernadette and tried to compare her age with hers. She did not know Bernadette's age but she was definitely older.

Bernadette, oblivious of the havoc she had wrought with her news, was busy selecting and displaying a number of wrappers for her customer to choose from. Madam Essin looked at her with envy. If Ralph were married, she would have had a grandchild or been looking forward to becoming a grandmother. Ralph's getting married was her main preoccupation since his return. But now she had herself to think about too. But thinking about herself was just like thinking about Ralph. For who was she without Ralph? It was like retiring with the knowledge that there was a competent person to take over. But was Ralph competent enough? Was he going to abide by her expectations? She had made all these expectations clear to him.

Her self confidence was slipping away and she felt indecently naked without the mask of confident assurance. Money and success were the tin gods of her existence. Now they were letting her down. She felt strangely dissatisfied. She felt a strong desire to see Ralph.

It was now two o'clock in the afternoon and Madam Essin felt uncomfortable. Something was nagging at her and she felt that seeing Ralph would purge it out of her system. The whole time she was in the shop, she had sold nothing. The few customers who had stopped to examine the *boubous* and lace materials had found them too expensive. They had not even given her the chance to try and convince them. Her irritability seemed to have contributed to this. Madam Essin finally decided that there was no need to stay. She collected her bag, locked her drawer and looked round the shop. Everything was in place. She knew she was going to find it the next day as she had left it. These were the things that were constant in her life. They never gave her trouble. They were not like children. People who wanted them did not always get them just like the clothes, which people wanted and some could buy and some could not. But unlike clothes, children are brought up and then in spite of all calculations and wishes, time and care produce results that seem mathematically incorrect.

She walked confidently up the stairs of the Ministry of Finance. She walked to the room where Ralph worked. The door was ajar but his seat was empty. When she enquired about Ralph's whereabouts, the man who shared the room with him told her that he was attending a meeting. As she stood there she imagined Ralph sitting in an air-conditioned room with a red carpet on the floor and chairs for visitors. She had entered many such offices when she was lobbying for this job for him. She quickly brushed aside these dreams when she realized that she had just been standing there. She explained that she had to see him because it was urgent. To make it look real she put on an expression of desperation as she swung her arms in despair and walked up and down the corridor. Theatricality was not beyond

Madam Essin if she stood to gain by it. The man walked to the end of the corridor, quietly opened a door and spoke to someone inside. He waited awhile for the response. Madam Essin frowned when the man conveyed the message to her. It was impossible for Ralph to see her. She interpreted this as his not wanting to see her and this made her feel more frustrated. So the meeting was more important than she was. She thought as she walked away. He will never want to see me again. She assured herself. She regretted this impulsive act since Ralph had told her never to come to the office to look for him no matter what happened. He knew his mother and did not want her to extend her domineering attitude from the home to the office. Now she had done just what she did not have to do. The situation was too much for her to pretend grace or elegance as she walked away. This was the breaking point. This was the last straw. How could he have told her such a thing and follow it up by refusing to see her? She wondered what had come over her son as she descended the stairs. Maybe it was that girl.

She arrived home at four o'clock. It was unusual for her to come back home so early. Sam had decided to go back to his room before coming back at five thirty before Madam Essin got back. She looked for her keys in her handbag and opened the door. Nobody had responded to her knock. The house was strangely quiet. She went to the stereo and turned it on. She was not really interested in the music. She just needed some noise for company. She opened her bedroom door and walked in, dumped her bag on the table and sat on the bed. At that moment her world came crumbling down on her. She could not bear the weight and gave in. She burst into tears. All the pent-up feelings fears and uncertainties of the past years, months and days poured out as she buried her head under the pillow. At first it was temper crying but it soon changed to a cry of general misery, a cry that had no nail to hit, no foundation, but a cry that enveloped everything, everybody. Her body heaved spasmodically as the tears ebbed and flowed.

The noise of the door opening brought her back from the pit of oblivion where she had taken refuge carrying along some of her despair, which in the other world turned into agonizing dreams she could not remember on waking up. She woke up with a good quantity of her despair still in control. By now she had become a mass of nervous energy, quick-tempered and intolerable. Sam's presence was just the right vent for it. Not unjustified to an extent.

"Where are you from? So this is how you leave the house. You go where you want and come back when you want. I see you are the master now."

Sam was taken aback at this outburst. There had been a break in the cordial master-servant relationship since Ralph had left. Both of them had become highly strung for different reasons. Sam had been contemplating giving notice of quitting the job. He could not stand the manner in which his boss was treating her son. This was a good opportunity. But not yet.

"Madam, I just went back home to…"

"I do not pay you to go back home and do your own things," she shouted at him. Then she remembered the dusty cupboard and table. "You do not do any work in this house anymore. Even the cupboards and tables are dusty." She turned to look at them.

"They are clean Madam."

"They were not clean in the morning. If you don't want to…well…is there any food?"

"Yes Madam, let me warm it. Sam walked out of the parlour and Madam watched him. There was something different in his gait. That reluctance towards an obligation was obvious. She knew that she still needed him and was not ready to part with him yet.

Sam too was quite aware of this and took his time. It was a long time since his wages had been increased. He had not asked for it when Ralph came. Now that he had gone he wanted it to be maintained.

The food was placed before her and she ate without knowing what she was eating. Her mind was elsewhere. A look of self-conscious uncertainty crossed her face as she ate. She no longer felt the self-possession, which had been so much part of her. That was to be expected after the shock of Ralph's revelation and his consequent departure. What she did not expect was the lethargy this created in her, in spite of her determination not to allow events to drown her. While the mind concentrated on her thoughts, it did not watch the movement of food from her mouth to her gullet. A particle of food missed its way and went down the wrong path. She choked on the food and rushed to the toilet to discharge what was in her mouth. The coughing came in unremitting spasms and she coughed until her sides ached. After a drink of water, the cough abated a bit but still rakingly forced its way through her body. She sat on the chair and tried to catch her breath. When she blew her nose, oil was mixed in the mucous. It might have gone into her brain, she feared. Sam who had given her the glass of water stood by and watched helplessly. He did not utter even a word of consolation. He could not believe that the distance between life and death was just a hair's breath. He had never seen her in such a helpless state. She stayed very quiet after each fit of coughing as if the slightest movement would provoke it. She kept her eyes closed and gently breathed in and out. She stretched out her legs and allowed her body to relax. She sat for about five minutes just listening to her body. The fit of coughing had gripped her chest in such a manner that she thought she was going to die. As she sat there she made a resolve. Never was she going to weep again. It was a sign of weakness. She had to be strong not only for her sake but also for Ralph's. She wondered whether she had gone mad to allow herself to sink so low. She got up from the chair and went to her room. She gazed at her reflection in the mirror as if she was trying to decide whether the woman she saw there was the one likely to have taken leave of her senses. No. Not Perpetua. In her heart she told the woman in the mirror that problems should be faced and dealt with, not clouded by tears and emotions. She forgot to include the word "reasonably."

"Sam! Sam!"

"Yes Madam!"

"Do you know where Claudette lives?"

"Yes Madam."

"Go and see whether she is back from work. Tell her I want to see her this evening. Hurry."

"Yes Madam."

And her mind went to work planning her next move.

Claudette was back with her circle of friends. Her brief interlude of flirting with Ralph had not borne any fruits. It was not out of character and principle for her to maintain a cordial relationship with a male friend when everything else had failed. This approach to life had won her a good number of men friends. She was the type of girl who could comfortably fill in the extra place just to keep an extra male company. She believed that this would lead her to her man. Life springs such surprises she kept telling herself. Her mother had often rebuked her for her easy friendships with boys. Throughout her school life she had always preferred their company. This had worried her mother who believed that a girl should not expose herself so much to boys. But being the only female in a family of five children this was to be expected. Having to play and fight with boys from a tender age, an innate assertiveness had instilled itself in her. The desire to make her point and stand by it and to dominate was intricately woven into her daily words and actions.

She was once engaged to be married, but this had failed. The young man was the eldest of two sons in a family of six children. The boy was a civil servant but still lived in his parent's compound because there were many rooms there. Some were rented out but he could occupy some of them if he wanted. It was more convenient for him because he was free from paying rent and still had the privilege to occasionally eat from his mother's pot. Claudette did not like this dependent attitude. His parents dominated his life and everything he did was in line with their wishes and expectations. This exasperated Claudette who often found herself in conflict with them.

She had come to admire Madam Essin when she discovered that she was a woman of her own heart. She took situations into her hands when it came to making decisions. They were birds of a feather. For now her friendship with Madam was too valuable for her to ignore. She was the sole link to what she was still looking forward to, and if she were strong enough as she thought she was, to use her influence as a mother to whatever extent, then things might still work out for her. But for now she had to live her life.

Staying at home that evening was not the prospect she was looking forward to. She was ready to occupy herself with whatever diversion came her way. While waiting for the man who would make her his bride, she always had someone on the sidelines. Presently, her regular was out of town and as she sat in the taxi going home her mind was preoccupied with what to fill the evening with until sleep overtook her. Her best bet was to visit a colleague and spend the evening with her. About fifty meters from her house she saw Sam flash by from the direction of her house. She asked the taxi driver to stop and she got out. Instinctively she felt that he had come to look for her.

"Sam, were you looking for me?"

"Yes, Mademoiselle Claudette, Madam sent me to tell you to see her as soon as you return from work."

While he gave the message he did not look at her. He might have been speaking to someone behind her. It did not matter to him whether she got the information or not. Her general behaviour when she came to the house did not please him. He did not equally approve of the manner in which his boss and this girl were treating Ralph whom he had come to love like a brother. He made to continue on his way.

"Sam please wait. Thank you for coming to inform me. Tell Madam I will come as soon as I change my clothes and eat some food." She rummaged in her bag.

"Take this and pay your taxi back." Sam took what she held folded in her palm. Some distance away when he opened his palm and saw the money the frown on his face deepened.

"Five hundred francs," he muttered to himself. "This is all she can give. If she thinks she can bribe me to her side, then she is wasting her time." The last part of her statement had pleased him because he did not want to be sent back to the kitchen again for her sake.

Since Ralph had declared his independence by moving out into an unfurnished apartment, events had moved too fast for Claudette to cope with. She did not know where Ralph had moved to and dared not find out because she had no tangible reason to go looking for him. She had decided to keep away from Ralph for some time to give his mother enough time to work on him. But she was going to make the best of this situation not only for Madam Essin's sake but for hers as well. In addition to this, she was dying to see this girl who was causing her friend so much misery and blocking her own way. If she did not succeed in reconciling Ralph and his mother through her getting married to him, then she was going to cause a disconcerting situation for the other girl. She was going to do it in such a way that things would never be the same again for the two of them. With Madam Essin's blessings things were going to work.

Ralph did not want to see his mother, at least not in the office. He was not sure of how he would react at her presence. Elise was still in town and that was his main preoccupation. He was determined not to have anything distract him He had tried his best to make her stay in Cameroon but wondered what he had to offer her. On second thoughts he agreed that her decision was inevitable.

He had felt strangely empty when he had finally accepted this fact. His mind had accepted the situation but his emotions still had to be convinced. He had planned to meet Elise that evening but he still had a long way to go to master his emotions. He wanted a perfect evening with her, an evening of peace and understanding, an evening during which he was going to get back Elise's love and confidence. Whatever the situation was, he did not want to miss this opportunity. Whatever he felt for her was built on an indivisible foundation. It was the type of love that had no recompense. He was not yet sure of what they were going to talk about or do. But he wanted to be alone with her, to sit near her and hold her. Now he had a sister. Yes he had a sister. He tried to summon up how one feels towards a sister one cherishes. All he felt was a confusion of emotions in the midst of which he assured himself that he must make her happy if only for this one evening. Making her happy would mean making himself happy too. But how was he going to prevent the knowledge of what had passed from clouding their evening together? Ralph set out planning what they were going to do but soon his mind started wandering.

He sat at his table pretending to be busy. It was 5 pm and his colleagues were leaving the office. But he stayed behind pretending to read some papers. He did not want to go back to his empty room neither did he want to go to his mother's house. He was hungry but did not feel as going anywhere to eat. Though he was looking at the papers, his mind had gone back to the day he had first met Elise. Physical attraction had led to a deep love, which he had to restrain. He examined the many opportunities he had missed in making love to her. His plastered leg was a great handicap. But the day it was removed was the best opportunity but he had let it go. He wondered why. He was drowning in the memories of that day. Elise had looked so vulnerable that he did not want his actions to be misinterpreted. He wanted her to accept him and offer herself willingly to him. Although he had regretted missing this opportunity on looking back he was glad he didn't do what was on his mind. As his mind kept on exploring his relationship with Elise he knew it would be impossible to get her out of his system. When her smile flashed across his mind he felt a warmness flow across his loins. He did not feel ashamed about it. The knowledge that they were blood relatives had not yet taken root. For now he did not want this to block his mind. It was a new emotion that he still had to master.

He wondered why he had confronted his mother the way he had if he had not wanted to recognize her as such. Was it a way of paying back what Elise had done for him? Was he trying to protect her from his mother? Was he trying to shield her from her own fears or he just wanted to vindicate himself of the evil his mother had committed, thus clearing both of their consciences?

Ralph was deep in thought and did not realize that everybody else in the adjoining offices had left. It was five thirty and he still had one and a half hours before meeting with Elise. He left the office and locked the door. He did not go to his room because he had the impression that his mother would be waiting for him there. But he had nowhere else to go. He took a taxi for the Kalafatas Bakery. He bought some cakes and two yogurts. As he sat at the veranda and ate he wondered why he found it so difficult to get interested in another girl. He was realizing more and more the grip that Elise had on him. There was not much he could do about it but he was certain that only one thing

150

was going to set him free. The possibility of it came to him as he opened the door of his room and walked in. He did not allow it to take root. The evening was going to tell. He fell asleep as soon as his head touched the pillow.

Elise was looking down at him on the bed. She was smiling down at him. It was that typical nurse to patient smile that made her look so cool and self-assured. She had on that gaze that made his loins hot. She turned to go, her white cap and uniform blurring his vision.

"Elise," he called and she turned and looked at him.

"I must go. The other nurses are waiting for me," she told him as she turned again to look at him.

"I want you Elise." He stretched out his hand to her, looking straight into her eyes, willing her to come to him. She took one step and stopped. He smiled at her, encouraging her to take another. But she stood as if transfixed, staring at him her eyes narrowing into dark pools. The room became dimmer. Whether it was from the sun's rays suddenly moving away from the window or he was drowning in the dark pools of her eyes Ralph could not tell. All he was aware of was the ticking of a clock. The indeterminate light in the room did not betray the time of the day. It was neither morning nor afternoon nor evening. The room seemed to be hanging somewhere up in time. Very little sound penetrated from outside and these faint impressions impinged vaguely on Ralph's consciousness. He was concentrating on the dark pools, which were pulling him deeper and deeper into its labyrinths.

His patience was running out. His body was getting hotter. The Plaster of Paris ceased to exist on his leg. It was like part of his leg. He held her close, kissing her passionately. Why had I not done this earlier he asked himself as his hands stroked her back gently and caressingly? He was on fire and his manhood was straining against his pyjamas trousers. It was straining for release, straining for relief. The room was swirling as he plunged deeper into darkness. He groaned and got up with a start.

He was hot and perspiring. The bedclothes were damp and rumpled. The room was hot. He sat up and looked round with unbelieving eyes. His manhood was still firm and he felt

151

wetness on his lap. This evening will tell he assured himself as he went into the bathroom.

Living without parents and finally knowing that one existed was earthshaking knowledge to Elise. It rocked her existence and even her encounter with Madam Essin had not undermined the moments of exhilaration, which she felt. Now she was on her way to meet her father, but Ralph kept interfering in the flow of her anticipated contentment. What was she really going to do with him this evening? She wondered. He had insisted on taking her out alone.

10

*R*alph and Elise were standing at the Carrefour EMIA waiting for a taxi to take them to Central town. The evening crowd of students and workers was as thick as usual. They stood in a queue on the curve of the road. They waited for taxis coming from the direction of Cetic Ngoa-Ekelle and Melen. The chanted their various destinations as the taxis crawled by.

The sun disappearing behind the seven hills that surround the city of Yaounde still had its remnants streaming the sky, their glow suffusing the clouds and giving the atmosphere a feeling of smugness. The streetlights were already on and the lights from approaching cars made sweeping cuts across them like meteors on a bright sky. The dry harsh heat of the day was turning into damp heat as rain clouds gathered overhead.

Ralph had been holding Elise's hand and the close contact of their palms made them damp. To avoid waiting for long Ralph manoeuvred Elise to the very beginning of the queue. It was already ten minutes past seven. They had wasted more than twenty minutes waiting for a taxi. To the next driver Ralph offered more than the normal fare.

The restaurant Tigre, situated on the street that makes an intersection with the French Cultural Centre, was already full with customers. The electric grills outside were sizzling with roasting pork, chicken and mutton. Walking into the restaurant was like receiving a cool spray after a warm bath. The ceiling fans cooled the room to a comfortable temperature. There were tables for couples and others for four people. The tables for two were set up near the walls and those for four at the centre. The serving section was located on the right of the restaurant. This provides a vantage point for the stewards to watch as their products are being consumed.

As soon as Ralph and Elise entered he spotted a couple leaving one of the tables by the window. As they moved towards it a waiter bypassed them and cleaned it before they sat down. He asked for their orders. Elise did not know what to choose but thought that anything with chicken would be all right. Ralph asked for mutton. Another waiter came to ask for their choice of drinks. Both of them asked for soft drinks but Ralph asked for a bottle of Chateau D'Anjou after their meal. While they drank the soft drinks and waited for their food, Elise looked round the restaurant. Ralph did not take his eyes off her face. He looked at her closely, noting the shape of her lips, the movement of her eyes as they moved round the room, the changes of her countenance as her mind reacted to what she was seeing. From the corners of her eyes she noticed that Ralph was looking at her intensely. A smile was creeping to her lips and she tried without success to suppress it. She did not want to be the first to speak. But a smile is sometimes the preamble to speech.

"What are you smiling at?" Ralph asked.

"Nothing."

"You cannot be smiling for nothing. What is on your mind?" Ralph insisted.

"Why do you want to know what is on my mind? It will not be of any interest to you."

"Just try me. You will be surprised."

"I will not say. You have been watching my face since we came in here. What is on your mind too?"

"I will tell you. I was thinking of the day I opened my eyes from sleep and saw you standing by my bedside like an angel." Then he laughed and held her hands across the table. She looked at him with an incredulous smile on her lips.

"You were not asleep. Your were wide awake when I first came into your room."

"But that does not change the fact that you were Godsend. I always thought about you and dreamt about you." He paused and added, "I still do."

Elise did not want to look at those honest eyes because she did not want to betray herself. Her skin pigmentation hid the flush that rose to her cheeks but her eyes were not so pigmented. Ralph saw the look in her eyes and understood. Their food arrived and they started eating.

Ralph took up a piece of mutton with his fingers. "Please do me a favour." And he brought it towards her mouth. Elise was embarrassed but since she did not want to draw attention to themselves she opened her mouth and took it.

After chewing she asked, "Why did you do that?"

"As a sign of my love for you. Here is wine for us to celebrate. I want this evening to be special for the two of us."

The food, drinks and general atmosphere in the restaurant made Elise really relaxed. She wanted to enjoy herself and she was doing just that. The conversation drifted to the nurses in the Bamenda Provincial Hospital who had attended to him. He could remember every one of them by name. They talked about his stay in Bamenda. Another past lurked beneath these reminiscences but neither of them dared bring it up. Ralph did not want to spoil the evening and made a deliberate effort to keep that past from his thoughts. Elise did not want to talk about it. After all she was going to leave all behind her. Ralph was bent on recapturing the moments he had spent with her. He dwelt on them, especially the ones he knew she had enjoyed most. He remembered these occasions in detail because they had meant so much to him. Suddenly he remembered how he had touched her paper cap and it had fallen off. Memory of her embarrassment made him smile.

"Why are you smiling? Elise asked. "You do not want to share your sweet memories with me?"

"Why do you say they are sweet?"

"If they are not sweet, you would not have been smiling."

Ralph did not want to remind her of this event and tactfully avoided responding by pouring wine into her glass with such concentration that it seemed he was afraid to touch the rim of the glass with the nozzle of the bottle. He then lifted his glass for a toast. Elise lifted hers too.

"Let us drink to..." he could not continue. His mind suddenly went blank. What was he about to say? The events of the past days were enough to unnerve a sensitive person like Elise. Ralph did not want to spoil the evening so he kept quiet.

155

"Let us drink to what?" Elise asked.

"Let us drink to our love." He finally declared.

"What love are you talking about Ralph? When you know…"

"Stop it Elise! Stop it! We came here to enjoy ourselves. I still love you whether you want my love or not."

He bowed his head and picked at the food on his plate. He picked up his glass and sipped his wine all the time keeping his eyes away from Elise's penetrating gaze. What was the use? Elise thought. Going back to the past to destroy the present was not the way to help the future. She placed her palm on Ralph's hand lying on the table. The tension that was rising in them cooled off.

"Russell wrote to me," Ralph began as if they had been speaking about Russell. "I am thinking of spending a weekend in Bamenda." The smile was back on his face. The past was brushed away but not wiped away, for Elise was a concrete presence from the past. Ralph wanted a part of the past to complete the present. Elise was not interested in the past. To her, only the present mattered. She changed the topic.

"The wine is good. It adds taste to the food."

"I'm glad you're enjoying it. We will go home from here. I will get another bottle, so we may continue the celebration." Elise made no response to this as she ate the last grains of rice from her plate. She had enjoyed the meal. The wine was warming her body and in spite of the swirling fans in the ceiling there was perspiration in her armpit. She was feeling good, as good as she always felt when she was with Ralph.

They were in a taxi going home. There was one passenger in the taxi when they got in so they had the backseat of the taxi to themselves. Ralph's arm went round her and she nestled against him. Ralph cradled her and put her head on the crux of his neck. His palm was caressing her side. In this position, all that they felt for each other was flowing from one to the other. Elise had never felt so happy and contented. This was what she had always wanted and nothing was going to take it away from her. She was going to savour it to the end.

Ralph was busting with excitement and anticipation. His desires were materializing and he wished that no other person should enter the taxi and disturb this bliss. It was in this state of mind and body that they left the taxi and went into Ralph's apartment.

She stood for some time in the sitting room trying to control her emotions. All she noticed was that the room was bare. She was surprised for a moment, then grasped the situation and asked no questions. Ralph led her into his bedroom. This room was a big contrast to the sitting room. There was a thick carpet covering the whole floor. A large bed dominated. An open wardrobe lent character. The feeling of the room was one of a man's room. Coats and shirts hung in the wardrobe. Four pairs of shoes peeped from under the lace curtain that shielded the clothes in the wardrobe. This together with the window curtains was the only decorative trimming that softened the austerity of the room. A packet of air freshener hung at the edge of the only window and lent a fresh sweet smell to the room as the open louvers allowed draughts of air in. This made the room cosy and Ralph's personality was reflected in the room especially by the scent of the air freshener. It was unlike the sitting room, which still waited for Ralph to furnish it with things that would reflect his personal taste. She was surprised that Ralph's mother had not yet furnished the whole apartment.

Ralph guided her to the bed and made sure she was comfortable by taking away her handbag. In her tension and excitement she had held onto the bag as if by letting go she would lose something she cherished. He sat beside her and continued to caress her. He turned her to face him and brought his lips to hers. He kissed her gently. He released her and looked at her face to see how she was taking it. Her eyes were closed. Then he kissed her passionately, using his tongue to open her mouth. He could feel her gripping his shoulders more firmly and returning his kisses. He was gently pushing her onto the bed. She was beyond resistance and slowly slumped onto the bed.

"Your dress will be rumpled. Why don't you remove it?

Elise was absorbed by the warmth and did not want the spell to be broken. Her eyes were closed as she tried to capture and immortalize that moment. Ralph began to unbutton her blouse. She turned round to make the task easier but did nothing to assist him, for fear of breaking the spate of desire that was building up. She did not want anything to interrupt it. She was afraid that her body might betray her leaving her empty, defeated and dissatisfied. When her clothes were all off she still felt warm as Ralph had kissed every inch of her body as he undressed her. Her whole body was responding to his attention. To Ralph, every move was like a ritual that allowed him to explore, enjoy and understand what lay within this quiet and beautiful person. His eyes and emotions were opening to things which at first he had just imagined. He could not believe that Elise being so quiet and sensitive could respond so passionately. Elise knew she was a novice but depended on how she felt for him and how her body was reacting to make the right moves. As Ralph worked on her she clung desperately on him. By now her loins were on fire. She felt waves and waves of warmness engulfing her. Ralph was franticly sucking on her nipples as if he were a baby. She could feel him hard against her thighs. She was ready to receive him.

At that moment, there was a knock at the door. She was not sure that she had heard well. It came again. Ralph stopped momentarily in his kissing, and then he continued as if he had not heard. The knocking became persistent. They could no longer ignore it. It was coming at regular intervals as if the person knew he was in the room and was not ready to give up until he opened the door. Ralph was at first irritated by the knocking, but when he heard the voice at the door his irritation turned into anger.

"What do you want Claudette? I have had enough of you and my mother. You want to pursue me even here? I cannot fall in your trap. Both of you are wasting your time." Ralph sat up undecided on what to do.

"Do you want me to tell her that?" Claudette replied. "Ralph be a gentleman and let me in so we can discuss."

"We have nothing to discuss." Ralph was in a rage. He turned to look at Elise and their eyes met. Elise's head was resting on the raised pillow and she was listening too. She could not understand what was happening. It sounded like the continuation of an argument.

"Ralph please let me in. I have a message for you from your mother."

"I do not want to hear anything. I am not interested in whatever you have to say. Please go away."

There was silence from outside. Ralph lay back on the bed and held Elise to continue what he had been doing before he was rudely interrupted. Elise allowed herself to be kissed but the spell had been broken. All the excitement and anticipation had drained out of her. She looked at Ralph not knowing what to ask. The mention of his mother had brought back memories of their last encounter. She placed her face on the pillow and tried to obliterate the thoughts and images building up in her mind. Ralph continued kissing her body and murmuring words of endearment. But Elise was far away. A certain pang of jealousy gripped her and her thoughts took off on a different tangent.

"Who is she?" Elise whispered.

"I see you are not alone." Claudette said from outside. Both of them had thought she had gone away. She continued, "I now understand why you cannot open the door."

"Who is she?" Elise asked again looking with interest at Ralph, trying to understand something from his face. Ralph's rage turned into confusion. How was he going to explain this new situation to Elise? He sat quiet trying to master this new situation and his emotions.

"Claudette, I have told you to go away. I have never been interested in you and never will be." This fanned the flames of the fire that had been smouldering in Claudette.

"Are you with your ward servant I have heard so much about? I am really sorry for you Ralph. You have no head."

Ralph got up to open the door with the intention of giving her a slap on the face. There was all evidence that the ensuing scene would not be a pleasant one. Elise held him back. Her firm grip on his hand cooled the anger in him a bit. He sank back on the bed heaving with restrained anger. He could not look at Elise.

159

"Who is she?" Elise asked the third time. She was more confused than before. The reference to her rang a bell and the echoes kept re-echoing in her mind. She adjusted her position on the bed to have a better view of Ralph's face and see how he was taking all this. In the silence that followed her confusion drained away heavily and reluctantly. In its place was emptiness. It was the type of anticlimax that does not bring catharsis but waits for the inevitable. Elise waited for an explanation, which was just the logical successor to what had happened.

Claudette's footsteps could be heard receding. It seemed as if she was making it clear to those within that she was really going away. The silence that descended on the room was electric. It seemed to be vibrating from some inner force of its own. The noises outside were rushing in to occupy, to fill the vacuum. For some time, the distant murmur of vehicles driving past became the dominant noise in the room. It was like the tense silence that follows the announcement of a calamity to be followed by an uncontrollable outburst. But there was no outburst. An unexplained weariness descended on Ralph. He lay back on the bed, stretched his legs, heaved a sigh and stared at the ceiling. He seemed to be unaware of Elise lying beside him.

He was overwhelmed by the many crisis he had been facing since he came back. First there was his accident, then his mother's dislike of the first girl he falls in love with. There was also the revelation of his relationship with Elise and now Claudette's determination to get him with the complicity of his mother. For the first time he regretted ever coming back. If he knew things were going to be like this, he would have stayed back in France and looked for a job. In his despair the idea of remaining in France was so appealing that he cursed himself for being such a fool. He was sinking into the depths of despondency when a slight movement of Elise's leg brought him back to reality. It was hard to bear all of these. It was even worse because not only had he to bear the problems he also had to go through the painful process of explanations. Instead of one he had two situations to explain to Elise. Unfortunately he was a man and not a woman. Women can cope with problems better than men because when situations become overwhelming they can have a good bout of weeping to release the tension that had been building up. Ralph as a man was not imbued with this quality. He mastered himself, heaved a sigh again and once more prepared himself to embark on another explanation, which he found painful and unpleasant. He felt a certain pang of guilt that he was responsible for dragging Elise into all of this. He started speaking to her softly and modestly but not timorously. All the time he spoke to her, he concentrated on the ceiling, his eyes intense, their dark centres and white surroundings standing out clearly under the glare of the lights. Elise had propped herself up on the pillow and was watching his face as he spoke. His words did not penetrate her thoughts and feelings. His words and her thoughts were moving on a parallel line with no intention of intersecting. She realized that her leg was still in contact with his and made no effort to remove it. Instead she threw her arm across Ralph's chest and pulled him to her. He stopped mid speech and turned to her. The smile on her face swept over him like a cool breeze on his hot conscience. It immediately cooled off all the words he thought were going to save him. They clung to each other for a breathless moment. Then she disentangled herself and got out of bed. At that moment she realized there had never been love between them that could make a marriage. Theirs was the stuff that dreams are made of. It was never of cold hard fact and passionate reality. It had been too gentle and kind, emanating from a deep sense of loneliness grasping and trying to keep an elusive longing and the desire to fill the vacuum that existed in them.

Carrefour Obili, the neighbourhood of Anglophones in Yaounde, is the name given to any visitor for easy identification of this area. In actual fact it is a rendezvous point. It is the place where friends and relatives saw off those going to the Western and Northwest Provinces. It is the place where people waited anxiously for people coming from these two provinces. It is the place where the long transport buses of Guarantee and Amour Mezam Bus Services slowly crawled round to make a U turn before coming to stop at their stations. It is the place where a sudden clash of metals was a daily sound. Two taxis collide. A sudden shout indicates that a pedestrian has been knocked down. This point is really a round about. But since very few vehicles enter or leave the street that enter into the neighbourhood, pedestrians and those waiting for taxis take the liberty to occupy the side streets. The way is open to vehicles coming from Central town to the Biyamassi neighbourhood and vice versa and then to other parts of the city. The many on license bars, provision stores, and women roasting fish, fresh maize and cocoyam by the road sides show the economic vitality of this area. Taxis arrived full and departed full.

Carrefour Obili is very busy in the morning. Primary school children, secondary school students, university students, civil servants, hawkers and market woman all gather here to get transportation to where they would earn a living either honestly or dishonestly. Carrefour Obili in the evening saw these same faces now looking tired, disappointed or satisfied. This morning, Rita was standing among the crowd waiting for a taxi to take her to Central Town where the offices are located. From a sense of economics taxi drivers took one or two people whose distances were long and many of those whose distances were short with the intention of making more money as they would drop many more passengers and pick others on the way before arriving the destinations of those with longer distances. Anybody going on a longer distance was expected to propose a fare higher than the one stipulated. Because of the crowd people who had short distances and wanted to go earlier proposed higher fares.

Rita was late. She was debating with herself whether to propose two hundred francs instead of one hundred francs. She worked at the Ministry of Finance and was anxious to get to the office early enough to treat some files before the file chasers came streaming along the corridors and tramping up and down the stairs. She had promised a civil servant who had come all the way from Idenau in the South West Province that his documents would be ready by 11 am that morning. He had really pleaded that he had spent three days in Yaounde and had to get back that day by the Guarantee bus that took passengers right to Victoria. She wanted her boss the director to sign the documents before he left for a meeting at ten o'clock. She was anxious to get the documents fast not only because of her promise but also because she was satisfied with the contents of the envelope that had been hidden among the documents. The owners of the other documents would have to wait until impatience would drive them to act accordingly or learn from the experience of others. She had needed the money in the envelope because she wanted to give Elise a treat before her departure.

It was eight thirty and Rita was still by the roadside. She had slept late the previous night. Her friend Elise had come back really agitated and had wept for a long time before falling asleep. She had stayed up trying to console her and find out what had happened to make her cry so much. Elise had not told Rita anything but Rita had concluded that whatever it was, it must have had to do with Ralph. She felt sorry for Elise and angry at the fact that she had not confided in her. She decided that she was going to get to the bottom of this mystery as soon as she got back that evening. She was prepared to confront Ralph if the occasion arose. Having lived in Yaounde for six years she was used to the whiles of men and boys. In a town where people fought for survival it was common for a boy to fall in love with a girl just to exploit her, and vice versa. She had learnt to stand on her feet and was ready to give any boy or man who tried to make her life miserable a good telling off. Thus she was not ready to see her friend made miserable by a man.

At one p.m. that afternoon, Carrefour Obili was less crowded. Taxis passed by with two or three people inside. Some were even empty. At this time of the day many of the clientele were at work but the taxis still moved around because in a city like Yaounde people are always on the move. The taxi men were no longer in a rush but crawled slowly looking for passengers. A taxi from the direction of Central town stopped in front of a shop at Carrefour Obili in which pastries are sold. A man got out but did not enter the shop. He walked for some distance back towards an entrance on the same side of the road that led to a neighbourhood that lay behind these shop front buildings. The road descended on a gentle slope. Ralph had come here the day Elise had arrived from Bamenda. He wondered whether he was going to find his way to the right mini-cite where Rita lived. At the bottom of the slope he turned left. As he walked he kept looking at the buildings. Soon he saw a closed gate painted white. He immediately recognized it. He felt elated.

He had promised to see Elise before her departure but he was not sure about how she was going to receive him. After Claudette's departure the previous night, Elise had left in anger though she had pretended she was all right. Ralph knew she was angry but there was nothing else he could say that could have wiped away the disappointment of that night. He was not sure whether Elise had believed him when he had tried to explain Claudette's presence. The whole morning in the office, he was restless and inattentive. He told his colleagues that he had not slept well. As he opened the gate and walked in he thought of what he was going to tell her.

The building was U shaped with all the doors opening to a common yard. The rooms were numbered but he had not taken note of the number on Rita's door.

He stood and looked round wondering which room was Rita's. Then he recognized the potted plant on the veranda with its tendrils climbing on the railings. He went immediately to the door and knocked. Elise was in the bathroom taking a bath. When she heard the knock, she was not sure that it was on her door so she turned off the flow of water to listen better. Ralph also heard the shower stop flowing and knocked again. Elise heard the knock well this time but turned on the water again. Whoever was at the door was going to wait or go away. She knew nobody in Yaounde who would come looking for her at this time of the day. Ralph had no choice but to wait. When the shower finally stopped flowing, he waited for five minutes and knocked again. Elise had thought that whoever was at the door had gone away. The knocking irritated her and she asked in a brusque voice, "Who is there?" She knew that Rita could not have come home so early. Even if she did, she would not only have knocked at the door, she would have shouted for her to open the door. At her question there was silence. Then he knocked again. Ralph was afraid that if he betrayed his presence, Elise might not open the door. Elise was really angry now and moved to the window to see who was outside. Ralph saw the blinds move and came to stand opposite her. Only the window separated them. Their eyes met through the slits in the window louvers. Elise had been debating with herself whether to see Ralph again or not. She had seen him and he had seen her. She could not leave him standing outside. His persistent knocking was indicative that he was not going to leave that easily. As she looked at him through the window, her resolve melted and she went and opened the door. Ralph walked in before Elise realized the enormity of what she had done. She never wanted to be alone with Ralph again for fear of what might happen. But after some thoughts she was consoled by the fact that this was Rita's room and Ralph would not dare try to repeat the events of the previous evening.

Ralph came in and sat down. Elise also sat down. It was as if they were meeting for the first time. They were uncertain about each other. A wall had descended between them. Ralph knew he had lost Elise's confidence. The knowledge that they were blood relatives had made their situation more complicated. He knew that Elise loved him to the extent of giving herself to him in spite of this knowledge. But the manner in which this love and confidence had been bruised was painful. Elise was leaving the next day. He did not want her to leave in the mood in which she had left his house the previous day. What he wanted to tell her could not also be said in a public place. He began.

"Elise, I have come to apologize for what happened yesterday."

It sounded so ambiguous. Elise wondered whether he was apologizing for what happened or for what had not happened. She made no response and he continued.

"Claudette had no right to come knocking at my door the way she did. You heard what I told her. My mother is behind this. Please believe me. I have nothing to do with her."

Elise was thinking. If she was going to meet her father who was Madam Essin's cousin, then there was no need to be angry with Ralph. She was going away and he would be left behind to love whatever girl he wanted. Her relationship with Ralph was at an end. But what type of relationship did they have? She wondered. Were they not related, in fact, were they not second cousins? At this thought she saw a solution to her predicament and pursued it. Though she loved Ralph not as a brother, she had to put this fact first. It would smoothen over the rough edges of her emotions.

"Ralph you do not have to apologize. I am not angry with you. I only felt that you were hiding something from me. If you have a girlfriend, there is no need hiding it from me. Remember that we are related."

While she spoke, Ralph was looking at the floor. At the last statement he lifted his head and looked at Elise as if she had just made a pronouncement freeing him.

"You are right Elise. We are related. But that does not stop me from loving you. You are very special to me."

"I am glad to be special to you. But let this not disturb your life. I am leaving for Buea tomorrow. All I want to take along are sweet memories not disturbing ones."

"I want you to understand one thing Elise; you are the first woman I have ever really loved. I may love another woman when you leave but that will take time."

"That is just what I do not want to happen. You should be able to love another woman as soon as possible. It will be better if you continue with the girl who came knocking last night. She seems to love you so much" It was out of her mouth before she saw the expression on Ralph's face.

"Elise! Don't say that! I don't want to hear it. I have never loved her and never will."

Elise was shocked at this outburst and was happy that she had not had the opportunity to meet Claudette.

"I am sorry Ralph. I did not mean to provoke you. I understand. But you have to be strong. I do not know what your mother is up to."

At the mention of his mother, Ralph stiffened. For the second time he regretted ever coming back to Cameroon. His mother was making things difficult for him. Elise's complicated history was yet to be discussed. He wanted to talk about it. He wanted to know how she felt towards his mother. Since they had faced his mother together, Elise had been reticent about her feelings towards her. The few times he had tried to bring up the topic, he had noticed the pained look in her eyes and given up. But today things had to be brought out into the open. He wanted them to talk about his mother. She wanted them to talk about her father. This was the ideal opportunity for them to do so. But each of them did not know how to begin. When Ralph mentioned his mother, Elise avoided his eyes by looking out the window. She knew that a raw spot had been touched but this time she did not let go. She wanted to follow this to the end.

"It must have been her instinct that made her hate me so much without knowing who I am. I do not know what she did to my father. But there is one thing she cannot change. It is the fact that she is related to me. If this relationship did not include you, I could have denounced it."

Ralph's eyes were still down. He dared not look at Elise. He did not want to see the look in her eyes for it was evident in her voice. Her expression could not have been different from her voice. They carried a note of angry defiance. Then she changed her tone. Time was running out and she wanted to get over the big question that hung over her. Without any preamble she asked.

"Ralph, did you know my father?"

Ralph's heart fluttered. This was opening up old wounds. But Elise's voice was so neutral that there was no way he could escape her question.

"Yes, but I was a child then."

"Can you tell me how he looked?"

"You resemble him a lot. You did not see the expression on my mother's face when we went to see her. It was as if she had seen a ghost."

"What type of man was he?"

"Whatever I tell you will be from the point of view of a child. It might not be correct. He might not be the same person today."

"Just tell me."

"What do you really want to know Elise?"

"You might not understand Ralph. He is my father and I have never seen him. I am going to meet a man I do not know. So every little bit of information about him will help."

"Elise, I was still in the primary school when your father left this country. All I can remember is that he was good to me. He brought me sweets and biscuits whenever he came visiting. He had time to talk and play with me. I loved him like my own

167

father. My own father left me too. But at least I can remember who he is. All I am saying is that you take after your father. You are so simple and good, so unassuming. Your father cannot be different. I am sure he loves you. He wants you to be with him. Your decision to go and meet him is good. God alone knows why he does everything. From the type of person you are, I am sure you are going to make it with your father. It is because your father loves you that he wants you to be with him. I am sure of that."

"What did your mother actually do to my father?"

"All I know is that my mother did not want your father to marry your mother. But it is over. Let us not talk about it. We are young, our future lies ahead of us. Let us not talk about the past because it hurts.

"It no longer hurts me. I have been hurt so much so that I am no longer sensitive to pain."

"Elise, you are a sensitive person. You cannot be insensitive to pain either yours or that of others. You do not express it but it shows in your face. I am happy that we are talking about it at last. It is good. I have been hurt too. But that is not going to ruin my life. Let it not ruin yours."

"I am glad to have known you Ralph. I am glad I was given the opportunity to be good to you. Can you imagine how I would have felt if I had known all this when you were hospitalized in Bamenda?"

"Don't imagine Elise. That is what is going to hurt most. You could have been forced not to be your real self."

"Thank God things have turned out the way they have. Though I am still on the precipice I am no longer afraid of the abyss."

As they were speaking they heard approaching footsteps. They paid no attention to it because it could have been going to the neighbouring rooms. But the footsteps kept coming towards the door of Rita's room. From the rhythm of the steps Elise imagined they could be Rita's. But it was not yet closing time and Elise could not think of any reason why Rita should come home so early. It was Rita, and Elise and Ralph waited for the knock on the door with a worried look on their faces. Ralph was not ready to meet Rita. Ralph looked at Elise's face and saw

168

the same confusion on it. As Rita approached her door she heard voices within. She stood still for a few seconds and opened the door without knocking. Two pairs of eyes looked up at her. She looked from one to the other. She was surprised to find Ralph in her room and her earlier antagonism started mounting. But the expression on Elise's face dispelled this. She was smiling. Rita came in and sat down. Elise began, "Rita, I am sorry for all the secrecy. I should have told you earlier but I was confused. I did not know what to tell you. But now I want to introduce you to my cousin Ralph Essin Bekayo. You might have thought he is my boyfriend. But he is not. His mother and my father are cousins. I did not know this when I met him in Bamenda."

Rita looked at them one at a time. She did not know whether to believe what she had been told or not. She turned to look at Ralph. But his gaze was focused on the floor before him.

"Is this true Ralph?"

"Yes, Rita. I am sorry that you are forced to be involved in this strange story. Elise and I are second cousins. At first we were lovers and I even proposed to marry her. Recent events and the past have changed everything. I am even more grateful that Elise is my sister rather than a girlfriend."

"I really do not understand what you both are talking about. I have known Elise all my life and I know all her relatives. This talk of cousins and aunts I have never heard of is hard to believe."

"I am her cousin on her father's side."

Rita's eyes narrowed in disbelief. Elise's father was non-existent. The family never talked about him. Now he had miraculously appeared, not alone but with a nephew and a big family behind him. They all sat quiet for some time, Rita thinking about the strange revelation, Elise about Madam Essin and Ralph about his uncle.

It was getting to three o'clock and Ralph had to get back to work before closing time. He was uncomfortable in the silence and looked at his watch. He wanted to get up, excuse himself and go. But he could not. He felt that he had to say something, some sort of conclusion to this strange conversation they had been having.

"Rita, I am sure that you have found this very strange. A child cannot be born by a woman alone. Elise has a father and that father has a family, a large one for that matter. She must have told you that she is going to meet her father. Her father is my uncle. She is your friend and I am sure you know her more than I do. So please help her get over this."

He paused for a while.

"Now that you know who we are, I think we should give a befitting send-off to Elise this evening. I will be here at 7 pm to take both of you out. Things have happened the way they have. Let us not allow it to affect our present and the future. This is an evening to celebrate and be happy."

He got up and straightened his coat. Rita had been looking at him as he spoke and when he got up to go she did not stop looking at him. Elise got up too. When both of them were outside, Rita got up and went into the room. She had to take off her shoes and clothes. Elise accompanied Ralph right up to the streets. They did not speak to each other but walked side by side. When they got to the street Ralph took her hand in his. Taxis were passing by but Ralph did not let go of her hand or make any effort to stop any. It seemed as if he did not want to go. Elise felt his warm palm in hers and thought of Ralph the patient in the Bamenda Hospital. It had been all so strange. She broke the silence.

"Ralph, you must go. We cannot stand here forever."

"Are you all right, Elise?"

"I am. Why do you ask?"

"I was just thinking…"

"About what?" she prompted him.

"I will tell you this evening."

He stopped a taxi got inside and offered two hundred francs to be taken to the ministry. Elise walked slowly down the slope. She felt light and relieved. She was ready to answer whatever questions Rita was going to ask. And indeed there were questions she was going to answer. There were questions that Rita wanted to ask but Ralph's presence had prevented her. Rita was sitting in the parlour when Elise returned. As soon as Elise entered Rita asked, "Did he really propose to marry you?"

"Yes he did."

170

"Did you accept?"

"Yes I did."

"When did you two know you are related?"

"My aunt told me when I told her about the proposal."

"Why did you accept to marry a man you hardly knew? If you had taken time to know him maybe this situation would not have arisen."

Elise sat down. Rita sounded as if she was blaming her.

"I loved him Rita. Is that not enough grounds for marriage?"

"No, Elise. So you can marry a devil just because you love him?"

"Ralph is not a devil."

"I have not said that he is. I am just trying to tell you that love is between two families and not between two individuals. However it is over."

They sat quiet for some time. Rita was still inquisitive. There were many things, which she still wanted to know.

"Have you met his mother?"

Elise felt irritated by Rita's continuous questioning. But she had decided to answer all her questions. It would straighten out the little tension that had been building up in the relationship between them because of her evasiveness. Moreover no harm would be done if Rita knew all that had been happening. She responded, "Yes I have."

"What did she say? Did she know that Ralph wanted to marry you?"

"I do not know. But from her face I could see she was not happy to see me."

"It's very strange. But I am happy you're going away. If it is true that she did what it is believed she did, then I do not know how you can face her again. How did you feel when you saw her?"

"I felt sorry for her."

"Sorry! Elise you are a strange girl."

"I did not really feel sorry for her. I cannot remember how I felt. But I found it difficult to be angry with her."

"So you forgave her?"

171

"I was too confused to think about anything. You know that whatever happened took place before I was born. So I cannot really say I know exactly what happened."

"How do you feel about Ralph now?"

"I still love him…"

"But not as before." Rita concluded.

"I am happy at the turn of events," Elise continued. "I do not know how I would have lived in Cameroon under the present circumstances. What is worse is the fact that there is a girl Ralph's mother wants him to marry."

"What!" Rita exclaimed. "How did you know about her?"

"Yesterday, while I was with Ralph in his room the girl came knocking."

"Did he open the door?"

"No."

"Did you see her?"

"No."

Rita was disappointed. This was getting interesting and she had been looking forward to a confrontation. Elise too was getting excited with the narration.

"What did Ralph do?" Rita pursued.

"He told her to go away. He told her that he was not interested in her and never will be."

"He did?"

"Yes then he told me that his mother was behind all this."

"Are you sure? Did you believe him?"

"Yes I did. Ralph cannot lie to me."

"You are so naïve Elise. You do not know what men can do."

"You do not understand Rita. What exists between Ralph and me cannot be explained. What can he gain by lying to me? He knew I was going away. He knew we are related."

"That might be the reason." Rita replied.

"There is no other reason. Things are just the way they are. And I want them that way."

Elise was weary of the question and answer session. Her voice indicated this. Rita took note and stopped her questioning. But she did not stop talking.

"This is your evening Elise. I think we should really celebrate the end of this nightmare. Ralph looks a very interesting person." Elise smiled at her friend.

A haze of smoke hung over the street. The glow from the street lamps was formed into misty balls of light with insects flitting in and out. Above this layer of lights, the heavens were dark. Below, lights from passing cars and nearby shops crisscrossed. But the smoke from roasting pork, chicken, fish and mutton still imposed murkiness. The Monte Cavour Street was busy. Both sides were filling up with cars. It was eight p.m. and this spot of nighttime eating and drinking was already busy. Early arrivals, their stomachs filled with flesh and beer, were already going away to give a chance to latercomers. Rita, Elise and Ralph came out of the taxi. Elise looked round and could not believe that so many people could come to one spot just to eat flesh and drink beer.

Ralph led the way and they entered the main building where the women had positioned themselves in such a way that customers could pass along the rows and examine and choose the type of flesh they wanted. The price of fish varied according to the size. Chicken was two thousand five hundred francs a quarter. Pork and mutton were one thousand francs apiece. The aroma that hung about the place made Elise's mouth water. They saw one woman who did not have many customers crowded around her and moved towards her. She was roasting fish. Ralph asked the ladies what they would like to eat. Elise asked for fish. Rita asked for fish too. To join the ladies Ralph asked for three roasted fish, the type known in French as "bar." The place was suffocating because of the heat and smoke. Ralph led them away along a passage to a room that looked like a sitting room. The upholstered chairs looked more comfortable than the table chairs found in the main hall where there were tables around which chairs had been arranged. But they were more uncomfortable when one had to sit on them and eat a whole fish and drink one or two bottles of beer. A waiter came and asked what they would like to drink. Elise asked for a bottle of Malta Guinness but Rita discouraged her saying that it was too heavy considering that they each had a fish to eat. Elise changed her mind and asked for a bottle of pamplemousse. Rita asked for the same. Ralph asked for a bottle of Coca cola. When the drinks arrived, Ralph served Elise first then he served Rita. He wanted to be the perfect gentleman. They took up their glasses and toasted Elise. Rita wished her a happier future. Ralph wished that Elise would not forget him. Elise laughed and promised never to forget him. They were being wonderful to her and she liked this very much. She felt really happy. The clouds that hung over her life had cleared and she was relieved. Ralph was very charming to the two women. There was no longer any reason for any ill feeling. As they sat drinking while they waited for the fish, the curtain made of beads parted many times with a clacking sound. Other people were looking for a place to sit. At one moment the curtain parted and the person did not go away. It was Claudette. She walked right in.

"Here you are Ralph. I saw you coming out of a taxi as I was going home. I knew I would find you here. So this is the queen?"

She looked at the two girls not certain which one was Elise. The two girls looked at Claudette then at Ralph. He almost choked on his drink.

"Claudette, what do you want from me? Why do you follow me wherever I go? I cannot stand it any longer."

While Ralph was speaking Elise whispered to Rita. Rita who had already been drawn to Elise and Ralph and who felt that whatever concerned them concerned her too, felt that she had to do something. She knew that Elise would not say anything and Ralph would not be able to handle the situation alone. She had to intervene.

"Who are you?" Rita asked.

"You want to know who I am?" Claudette asked piqued.

"That's what I mean. Don't you understand simple English?"

"You do not need to know who I am. I was speaking to Ralph and not to you."

"Oh I see. You are the girl who has been following Ralph around like a dog. Are you so thickheaded and shame proof that

174

you cannot realize when a man does not want you? If you cannot realize that then you can at least realize that Ralph has company. He is not sitting here alone. So behave yourself."

Elise was enjoying this and held her mouth to prevent herself from laughing. Ralph was so surprised at the way Rita was reacting and was also glad that he had been spared handling a situation he knew was going to be nasty.

"What I have to discuss with Ralph is none of your business."

"It is my business. You came bashing in here like a mad woman. I am not going to allow a mad woman to spoil our evening. We came here to enjoy ourselves and we do not want to be disturbed by a mad woman. So can you please walk out?"

Claudette was not prepared for such an attack. She had come with the intention of showing whoever Ralph was with that he had another girl in whom he was more interested. She had planned to use every trick at her disposal to get Ralph out of the room. But Rita's immediate attack had disarmed her and there was no room for her to try any tricks. Rita's attack had made Claudette believe that she was the one in Ralph's life and she responded with venom.

"I am not going to walk out. Not at your command."

"Then at whose command are you going to walk out. At Ralph's?" Then she turned to Ralph. "Ralph, please can you ask her to walk out?"

As if on cue Ralph asked Claudette to walk out. She was speechless and left the room without a word. But before she left she glared at them, bundled the string of beads that served as curtains and flung it at them. The beads clattered towards them and fell helplessly back in place. They burst into laughter. The sound of their laughter followed Claudette out onto the street.

While all this was going on, Elise kept looking at Claudette. She was definitely older than Elise and the grimace on her face as she spoke did not improve the situation. They were all relieved at her departure. Rita continued to laugh when the others had stopped. She was really amused at Claudette's sudden defeat. She had expected an exciting scene. But it had ended so quickly.

"Is that the girl who thinks she can marry you Ralph? She would have made a very miserable wife. You are too handsome for her to withstand advances from other women."

Elise was shocked and Ralph looked at her with disbelief. Rita continued.

"You may think I am crazy. But I am not as crazy as that woman who just left. What I am saying is the truth." Ralph looked at Elise and they started laughing again. The atmosphere was relaxed when the fish arrived on a single large tray. It was accompanied by pepper sauce and myondo. They washed their hands and started eating. The fish was tasty. They ate in silence, each determined to enjoy the evening in spite of what had happened.

11

*E*lise's journey to Buea was a replica of the last one. She was full of anxiety. She knew what she was going to do but did not know how she was going to do it. The tight knot in her stomach could not be eased by the thought of her impending journey. In her mind, she went through the letter she had written to her aunt. She hadn't the courage to tell her of her decision in person. She was afraid that her reaction would jeopardize her decision. She had gone too far to retrace her steps. There was much at stake, which she was not ready to risk. She had done everything to make the letter unassuming. She had examined every word and sentence assessing every possible reaction to it. It was a short letter. It was not as long as it could have been if she had written all she felt in it. If she had done this she might have unintentionally expressed how she felt. But keeping it short and to the point, she had finally accepted that this was a written representation of her thoughts. In the letter, she had written all that she wanted to get off her chest, and at the same time not what would hurt her aunt. She made it clear that the desire for a father was an innate tendency that could not be explained away.

She left Yaounde on the Guarantee bus that carries passengers straight to Victoria. She came out at Mutengene and took a taxi for Buea. When she alighted at Great Soppo and searched her bag for money to pay the taxi driver, she saw the letter she had written to her aunt. It struck her that she could have posted the letter. But she wanted to see her cousins again. She wanted to see her aunt too, but there was nothing for them to discuss. The decision had been taken. She was no longer in control of the events.

Her father had sent her an air ticket and she had collected the traveller's cheques before leaving Yaounde. Of the three hundred thousand francs sent to her, she had put one

177

hundred thousand francs in the envelope for her aunt. She had made a money order of fifty thousand francs in the name of Ralph Essin Bekayo. This she had put in an envelope to be posted at the airport. She made a gift of thirty thousand francs to her friend Rita. That morning she had bought gifts of dresses and shoes for her cousins.

As she sat in the bus heading for Douala, she tried to empty her mind and doze off. She had decided not to bother about anybody's reaction. Any reaction would not have her as a witness. What lay ahead of her needed all her wit and energy and what lay behind was passed and done with.

Elise arrived in Buea at eight fifteen p.m. on Friday. Her aunt had gone to a wake keeping at Small Soppo. Elise was grateful for her absence. The children were happy to see her especially as she had gifts for each of them. They put on their shoes and dresses and displayed them to her amusement. She advised them to remove the dresses and keep them to be worn on Sunday. She was not in the mood to play with them so they left her alone. The night was cold so she stayed in her room. As she lay on her bed and thought of her present circumstances, the enormity of what she had done dawned on her. She had single-handedly taken a decision. She had not as much as consulted with her aunt who was the only adult she could rely on. But she knew from what she had heard that such a step would jeopardize her dreams. She was not prepared for another painful confrontation. So she must go on with what she had started. It was her secret and she was determined to keep it so. She looked around the room. This was where she had grown up. She had slept on this bed for as long as she could remember. She soon fell asleep exhausted from the journey and the late hour at which she had slept the previous night.

Aunt Pauline came back the next morning at five a. m. She was the leader in their choir and they had to sing and dance all night at the wake keeping. She was exhausted and went to sleep immediately she got back home. The children were still asleep when she came back. But Elise heard as she opened the door and went to her room. She lay quiet waiting for her to fall asleep. Elise knew that she was going to sleep for at least two hours. This knowledge pleased her for she was going to succeed in her plan.

She knew her aunt would be anxious to know what had happened since she left Bamenda. Elise had not written to her despite her several letters warning her to be careful. It was one of these letters that had helped Elise make up her mind. Her aunt had told her that it was not going to be good for her to decide to marry a man without first consulting her family. She had wondered who her family was. The story was different before, but now that she knew she had a father who wanted her desperately, she had to do something.

Aunt Pauline did not know that Elise had made contact with her father. After coming back from Bamenda, she had thought much about what had happened in Bamenda. But her conviction of the impossibility of the whole issue had made it inconsequential. Yet she was anxious to know how Elise had handled the situation. Elise had not replied to any of her letters and this made her worry. She was also anxious to know how Elise felt towards her. She had the impression that a gulf existed between them. Their separation at the bus stop in Bamenda had been strained. She wanted to put things back in their right places, so she bided her time. She was fast asleep in her room not knowing that Elise was in her childhood room.

At six o'clock Elise got up from bed. The children were still asleep in their rooms. They always took advantage of their mother sleeping late on such mornings to also sleep. Deborah, the eldest, who was responsible for getting the children up from bed, was also sleeping. She knew that before her mother got up to scold her she would have enjoyed her sleep. When Elise got up and went to the bathroom to bath Deborah heard the noise in her sleep and thought it was her mother. She unconsciously covered her head with the blanket. Aunt Pauline was too deep asleep to hear any sound.

Elise, after bathing, quickly dressed. When she was ready to leave the house, she quietly went into her aunt's room. Her handbag was on the table where she had kept it the evening before. She lifted the bag and placed the envelope under it. Then she quietly left the house.

There was no rain. But it had rained up the mountain that morning. So there was water in the gutters and some had flowed onto the road filling the many potholes on this only street that leads in and out of Buea. Elise did not look about her. She concentrated on the oncoming taxis plying their way through the rough street down to the Mile Seventeen bus stop. One stopped for her and she gratefully sank into it. The taxi started its undulating crawl down the street. She had left her suitcase at one of the shops located at the bus stop and went to pick it up. She boarded a bus for Douala. Her flight was booked for one p.m. that afternoon.

Unlike Buea, Douala was flooded with sunshine. The sun had risen early as if to make up for the heavy downpour of the previous night. The sky overhead was blue but in the horizon were dark nimbus clouds that could in a moment spread into an overhead dark canopy leading to another downpour. By midmorning the intensity of the heat had increased. Combined with the humidity typical of the city of Douala, the streets were simply sizzling. The tarmac at the airport road was giving off vapour, which looked like solid sheets of heat as it was reflected off its surface.

Elise paid the taxi man she had hired to take her to the airport and stood looking around her. This was her first time of coming to the Douala International Airport. She was surprised at herself. She felt she could handle the situation. Without any directions or instructions on what to do she had to rely on her wits. She moved into the main lounge and watched to see where people arriving were drifting. She followed them and was soon in a line leading to a section separated by a railing. When she got to the man inspecting documents she did not know which ones were required so she gave him all her documents and her passport. He sorted them and gave some back to her. Then he carefully checked the ones that had remained in his hands. As he was doing this some other airport officials were checking her suitcase. There were just clothes and a few books. The weight of her luggage was not up to half of the limit. Soon she had to give way to the person next in line. She had noticed that those who had had their documents checked as well as their luggage were out of the barrier conversing with relatives and friends. Some

180

were eating and drinking soft drinks sold in the many snack shops that catered for the travellers and those who had come to see them off. Elise did not have any body to converse with. She was feeling quiet hungry and got herself a bottle of Coca Cola and a sandwich. As she ate she watched taxis drop people in front of the main lounge. The drink and sandwich finished she remembered that Ralph had promised to meet her at the airport. She wanted to see him before he could see her so she looked round for a spot where she could stand and see everybody who came out of any vehicle at the entrance. She positioned herself behind one of the pillars in the lounge. It was midday and she still had one hour to wait.

She became absorbed by the bustle around her. More travellers had arrived. She closely watched those who attracted her attention. There was this couple. They seemed to be newly wedded from the way they clung to each other. When she looked at their fingers there were no wedding bands to confirm this assumption. They were speaking in French and Elise could barely make out what they were saying. Her attention was soon diverted to a flashily dressed woman who walked into the lounge and went straight for checking in. Elise watched as she deftly produced her documents and seemed to wait impatiently as the official went through them. The expression on her face indicated that she was bored by the whole exercise. It seemed as if she had done it so many times that she thought it was just a waste of time, which she had to endure. As she gestured at her luggage, her fingers flashed with light. Eight of her ten fingers had gold rings on them. Her complexion was fair but the skin on her elbow knuckles and on her ankles betrayed years of complexion creams. Elise looked at the woman with awe. The man accompanying her was eclipsed by her flamboyance. Who was he? Elise wondered, husband or servant? She was engrossed in musing about the strange couple when by instinct she looked at the main entrance to the lounge. No vehicle had stopped to prompt her to look so she did not expect to see Ralph. It seemed the vehicle that had brought him had been parked at the parking space below and he had walked up to the entrance of the lounge.

Although Ralph had promised to meet her at the airport, when it got to midday and he had not arrived she was afraid that something might have stopped him from coming. She longed to see him before going away and could not imagine how she would feel if he did not come. From the events of her last night in Yaounde, she was sure that if he did not come his mother was responsible. With these thoughts she had prepared herself to accept any disappointment. But now that Ralph had come she felt relieved.

Ralph was walking determinedly towards the main entrance of the lounge. He looked neither left nor right. Elise watched him as he approached. His countenance was one of resignation under which a sort of tranquillity resided. His chin was clean shaven and his hair glittered in the sun. He was more handsome than she had ever seen him. His fracture had healed so well that there was no sign of it in his manner of walking to show that he had had that misfortune. He met a friend and they stood to greet each other. As they spoke Elise focused her eyes on him. She noted his every gesture and facial expression. She was mentally taking a last photograph of him. When he came into the lounge, he stood looking for her. She made no sign to attract his attention but stood with a beating heart for his eyes to find her. She was an easy target to locate in a crowd with her peculiarly dark complexion. The morning she had left Yaounde she had gone to a hairdresser and her dark luxurious hair was styled to fall on her nape in waves. Before she left Buea that morning she had taken some time to put on some makeup. Although her sweat had dampened the powder on her face, it heightened rather than destroyed the effect. After brushing past people, for it was getting to half past midday and the crowd had increased, he finally saw her and took her in his arms. She had prepared herself to make this parting as non-committal as possible. But as he held her she could not resist an impulse to hold him more closely. When he noticed the pressure of her hold increasing he also increased his. Soon both of them were panting slightly not from the effect of the embrace but from the emotions that coursed through them. After the embrace, they drifted away from the crowd.

182

"Elise, I am going to miss you a lot. I have never had a female relative as close to me as you are. Elise, I will always think of what you have done for me, particularly, the type of person you are. You are so selfless, always giving without asking anything in return. I am glad that God has given me a sister like you."

At the mention of the word "sister," her heart grew warm with happiness and gratitude from what he had said and from what she had come to feel. She believed that this new relationship was going to be more lasting than the previous one. The affection that goes with conjugal love can drift from one person to another, but the affection of a brother towards a sister cannot be transferred. It can only die. As they stood holding each other, Elise remembered what she had thought about the young boy and girl she had witnessed earlier holding each other. Anybody looking at them now would draw his own conclusion. With these thoughts she smiled.

"What is so amusing?" Ralph asked.

"Nothing?"

"You cannot be smiling at nothing. Don't let us start again Elise. There is no time to keep me in suspense. Now tell me why you are smiling."

"I am just happy. I am happy you have come to see me off. I am happy that I have a brother who cares about me."

In the course of telling a lie, she had told the truth of how she actually felt.

Unknown to them Madam Essin had also come to the airport. Claudette had narrated to her what had happened at Monte Cavour flavouring it with her own addition to enrage her. She did not tell her of how shamefully she had left them. Madam Essin was afraid that her son was going to spring a surprise on her, so she had monitored his movements and followed him to Douala.

The airport was now very crowded, for it was twenty minutes to one o'clock It took her some time to locate them. Her coming had been caused by her anxiety to see what her son was up to. But when she saw the two of them together, she hid herself to see what was going to happen next. As she watched them holding each other, she recalled that she too had once been a victim of such a situation. Having lost a husband whom she thought loved her, her feelings had moved from longing to anxiety, and then to fear. After receiving the letter that had pronounced the end of the marriage, her desire was to kill. If she had met him during that period, she would have committed murder. With the passing of the years this had turned into indifference. His existence was no longer part of her life. Since this break she had had other men in her life but she found it difficult to maintain any steady relationship for she was determined never to allow any man to interfere with her life.

Madam Essin stood watching the young people holding each other. She looked at the young man who was her son. How handsome he looked. When he smiled he had that elusive curve on his lips that reminded her of her husband. She had been unable to resist that curve of the lips even after eight years of marriage.

When her husband smiled she had the feeling he was looking down on her in amused condescension. This used to annoy her but she could not resist the charm he exuded. Now here she was an abandoned wife with an estranged son. Her thoughts roved as she watched them, plunging into the past, the present and the future. The girl brought back the past. She wished she could obliterate that past from her life and her son's.

As she watched them many thoughts went through her mind. Elise's going away was a relief to her. The curse on her would be lifted and more importantly she would have her son back to herself again, at least for a while before another woman took over. But this woman would be her choice of woman. The impulse to follow Ralph had overcome reason and she suddenly felt frightened of what would happen if Ralph found her there. She was not ready to face another scene. Memories of the last one drifted back to her and she tried to make herself as inconspicuous as possible.

The voice of the announcer came over the microphones requesting the passengers for flight number 747 of Swiss Air to get on board. There were last minute farewells. Some couples clung to each other as if parting was impossible. Ralph kissed Elise goodbye. It was a brotherly kiss. He held her for some time and then gradually released her. She turned and moved away resisting the temptation to look back. She did not want her expressive eyes, which were already laden with tears to betray her. She did not want to see his countenance but she knew he was looking at her retreating back. A last minute impulse to wave at him gripped her and she turned to wave. She glimpsed a familiar face in the crowd, which caught her attention. She turned in its direction. It was as if a spell had been cast over her. The expression on the face was indescribable. It had neither remorse nor joy, nor sadness or regret. It was just blank. Elise was so absorbed by the stare that she did not realize that she was obstructing the passage of the passengers who were going on board. As the passengers tried to bypass her they pushed her aside but this meant nothing to her. She kept her gaze on the face. She started moving towards the face and this caused more complaints from the passengers who cursed and nudged at her. But she did not mind and kept moving as if in a trance.

Ralph had been watching her and was now moving towards her, uncertain as to what was happening. He searched the faces in the direction towards which she was moving and saw his mother. He stood still and held his breath. His anger was rising and he hastened his steps to get to her before Elise did. But Elise got to her before him. She stretched out her arms and held Elise in a heartbreaking embrace. There were tears in her eyes. Ralph stood for a second watching them then he rushed over and enclosed both of them in his arms. For one suffocating minute they were united. Elise quickly broke away from the embrace and rushed after the last passenger. Her eyes were clouded with tears as she stumbled along. Her last look back found mother and son holding each other and waving at her. Madam Essin smiled as tears rushed down her cheeks. Elise gave them a brief wave and turned away. The picture of mother and son as they stood together was printed on her mind. This was the picture she kept in her heart. They were together again and happy.

As the plane took to the air, her tears together with the clouds in her view, gave her the impression that she was breaking through to another world. She lay back and tried to empty her mind of everything else. What lay in store for her beyond the clouds and what her reactions would be was an enigma.